Ellie Dwyer's
Big Mistake

Diane Winger

ISBN-13: 979-8619827439

DEDICATION

To Charlie:
"We're still having fun and you're still the one."

ACKNOWLEDGMENTS

I'm filled with gratitude toward my friend and editor, Val Burnell, for again helping me to hone my story and characters to their finest. My cover designer, Christine Savoie, has once again captured the mood of the book with graphics that will catch the reader's eye.

My husband, Charlie, is always a source of inspiration with his wild sense of humor and passion for adventure. Thanks to him for his bravery in reading and critiquing the first drafts of each of my books! His thoughtful suggestions always help more zest and passion into my work. Thanks also to friends Joyce Fischer, Cheryl Borchardt, and Beth Sholes for your inspiration and insightful feedback.

I'm grateful to my fellow campers and friends who have shared their experiences with me through social media. Several of their stories inspired scenes in this book. My thanks go out to Marsha Adams, Bob Bauer, Amy Jo Egress, Angela Morris Steelman, Mackie and Joyce Adams, Sara Anne, Peggy Kuba, and the Dowding family & Aidan, for your tales of being locked out of your camper, herds of deer in camp, campground beggars, summertime Santa, shower calamities, tornado bunkers, skunks, traffic jams, and more. I've applied a liberal amount of literary license, mixed in with my own experiences, to flavor my rendering of these vignettes.

Finally, many thanks to all my readers of this and my prior novels. I hope you've found them entertaining, inspiring, and worth your time. I appreciate the comments that readers send me, positive or negative, and hope to grow as a writer with help from your feedback.

Chapter 1

I sit back from my laptop with a deep sigh, removing my reading glasses and rubbing my hands over my face. Charli leaps down from her perch by the window of my little camper and *mews* at me, hoping for attention after all the time I've been ignoring her, working on my unusually tedious proofreading job. I glance outside and note that the rain has stopped, at least for the moment.

"How about we take a little walk over to your place, little one? We've been cooped up too long."

I pull on a raincoat in case the clouds open up again, slide my phone into an outside pocket, and open the door. The cat bounds down the stairs only to discover that the ground is sopping wet. Shaking her paws in disgust, she reverses course and tries to scamper back inside.

"Nope," I say as I scoop her up and place her on my shoulder. It's taken a while, but Charli now accepts me as a substitute perch when her "mom" – my best friend, Ruth – isn't available to carry her around. She wraps herself around my neck like a stole and purrs as I transport her to Ruth's more spacious camper just a few sites down from mine.

Just as I deposit her inside, the opening chords of "On the Road Again" fill the air – my special ringtone for Ruth.

"Hey there. How are the errands coming along?" I ask.

"Well, definitely not as planned. Actually," she says, drawing the word out, "I had a little mishap. A minor fender-bender."

"Oh, no! Are you okay?" Knowing Ruth, "fender-bender" could be significantly downplaying the situation. Last year a rock tumbled down a steep slope above the trail we were hiking along and struck her lower leg. She sat down and rested for a minute, then insisted she was fine and we should continue, waving me off when I wanted to take a look beneath her pant leg. I caught her later back at camp, icing a swollen and multi-colored bruise that looked like she had half of a baseball implanted in her calf.

"I'm fine. Just a bit of a sore neck. The problem is that they want to keep me overnight for *observation*." I can visualize her eye-roll on the final word. "Just because I'm so ancient, I'm sure."

By the numbers, Ruth is indeed old. But she's by far the fittest, healthiest eighty-two-year-old I've ever encountered. Still, I'm relieved the doctors are being thorough. I'm certain there's more that she hasn't yet told me, but I doubt I'll get the information out of her over the phone.

"So, what happened?"

She sighs. "You know, I was just waiting at a red light behind another car when this guy plowed right into the back of my truck. I suppose it could have been because of the wet road, but honestly, I think he just wasn't paying attention. My truck's back end is pretty messed up, so it's in the shop for a week or so. Anyway, the insurance company said they'd get me a loaner car, but that leaves me with the problem of how to vacate my campsite on Tuesday. I'm negotiating with them to lend me a truck with a hitch, but I'm not hopeful."

I hear a voice in the background. "Mrs. Erlich? I'm here to take you down to radiology."

Radiology? "Ruth, where *exactly* are you? What hospital?

2

I'm coming to see you." I dig a pen and scrap of paper out of the junk drawer in her kitchen, realizing that my hands are trembling.

"There's no need for that, Ellie. I'm sure I'll have a vehicle tomorrow and ..."

"Ruth, I'm coming and that's that. What's the name of the hospital?"

The nurse or technician or whomever speaks up, providing the directions I need. As usual, Ruth probably has her phone speaker on. "I'll be there as soon as I can," I announce to any and all listening.

Making sure that the cat is safely ensconced in her climate-controlled home, I lock up Ruth's camper and scurry back to my Jeep Wrangler, tap my destination into the GPS, and head out of the campground. Just as I'm about to turn onto the main road, my phone *pings* with a message. Thinking it could be a text from Ruth, I dig my phone out of the pocket of my purse in time to merely catch a glimpse of the message. It's from some person whose name is unfamiliar, but the preview disappears just as I think I've recognized the words *vanderwal ia* in the text. My heart skips a beat and I feel a bit queasy.

"Don't be ridiculous," I scold myself out loud. It's just my mind playing a trick on me because I'm stressed about Ruth's accident. How crazy to conjure up a buried memory that I've managed to suppress for decades! It probably said something like "wonder where i am" or "valuable item" or something else completely unrelated to Vanderwal, Iowa. Spam, most likely.

Forcing my thoughts back to the present, I check traffic again and pull out onto the road, focused again on determining my closest friend's true health status.

***

"You didn't need to come." Ruth's words say one thing, but her smile when I walk into her hospital room reveals something entirely different. How could I have possibly stayed away?

"I expected to find you in a neck brace," I say. I had also imagined an assortment of bruises, but none are apparent.

She touches her throat gently. "Just minor whiplash. They've been wrapping my neck in icy-cold compresses, but are giving me a break at the moment. I should get out of here by noon tomorrow. The good news is that the doc said I was amazingly fit and healthy *for my age*." She starts to shake her head to go with her eye-roll, but cringes in pain. "He told me that he wants my genes," she adds, grinning. "I told him they would be far too tight a fit on him."

Her sense of humor is still intact – that's a good thing.

"Listen," I say, "about moving on to our next campground. Why don't I make a few calls and see if we can extend our stay at Whispering Clouds for another week or so, and delay our arrival at the Crater Lake resort till later?"

"It's awfully late notice to stay on."

It'll be the middle of the week, and there've been vacancies in the campground ever since we arrived three weeks ago. Besides, the camp managers are enthralled with this petite, lively octogenarian – they love her. Everyone does. I'll bet they'll bend over backwards to help her out once they hear what's happened. "Let's see what I can do."

I look around her room, noting the cheerful yellow of one wall and matching cushions beneath the window, with contrasting blue and yellow striped curtains. Perfect choice for Ruth, who loves brilliant colors. "Nice décor," I say, as my memory conjures up a drab, colorless double room that was so typical of hospitals decades ago. Especially the one in Vanderwal, Iowa.

Damn. I thought I'd successfully pushed that distressing part of my life into the darkest recesses of my mind, never to be visited again. I'll just have to bury it all again. Focus on something positive.

4

"So, when do the doctors think you'll be up for hiking again?"

The corners of her mouth turn downward. "They said it might take between a week and a month, although I'm not supposed to just lie around, either. Not that I would." Her grin returns. "So, I figure I'll be ready in four or five days."

I don't doubt it. "Just listen to your body," I say, hoping she'll use a little restraint.

"My body is telling me it wants out of this place. It wants to be outdoors, or at least back at camp."

I lean over and give her a careful and very gentle hug. "That's my Ruth!"

It isn't long, though, before her body – surrendering to the pain medications and trauma of the accident – tells her it's time for a nap. I ease out the door in search of coffee.

Chapter 2

"What does that mean — a spot on your lung?" I was preparing to return to the hospital later this morning, expecting to bring Ruth back to the campground. Her phone call comes as a shock. I thought she was doing fine, other than having some sore neck muscles.

"It might not mean anything," she answers. "And maybe I'll still get out of here today. But I wanted to let you know not to make the trip back over here yet. Not until I hear more. They've told me someone will be taking me for a CT scan this morning, but so far I'm still just lying around waiting."

My imagination conjures up the worst. Lung cancer? Tuberculosis? Didn't Ruth tell me she once was a smoker? But that was ages ago — I think she quit when she was pregnant with her second child, so that's been what? Half a century ago?

Ruth sometimes jokes that she was named after Ruth Bader Ginsburg, the Supreme Court Justice. "We're both tiny, Jewish, and notorious," she says. "And both in our 80s, although I'm much younger than RBG." If my Ruth does, indeed, have cancer or another serious illness, I pray she'll emulate Justice Ginsburg and defeat it, determined to return to her active lifestyle.

"I'm still coming to visit, whether I get to bring you home

or not. I'll be there around noon. Oh, and good news on the camping situation," I say. "We're good to stay put at Whispering Clouds for another eight days." I don't mention that I'll need to move my camper/trailer to different sites twice during that time slot. The campground manager was able to juggle around one reservation for Ruth's spot so her unit can remain parked where it is, but with two different parties slotted for my site over that period of time, he wasn't able to do more than that.

I really don't mind. This has been an especially delightful campground, so the slight hassle of having to hook up, move, and unhook my trailer a couple of times is well worth the pleasure of extending our stay a bit longer. I was able to snag three more nights at the tail end of our reservation for our next location, less than an hour's drive from Crater Lake, so that will still give us about three weeks to explore that area. Hopefully, Ruth will be feeling up to enjoying all our planned hikes and the boat ride on the lake by then.

Now that the rain has passed through, the sky is the clearest I've seen in a week. Water droplets hanging from the leaves in the trees sparkle like crystals and the air is filled with the smells of rich, loamy soil and flowers. Like many of the other people camped here, I'm pleased to be able to resume my usual morning hikes around the campground loops, detouring onto the short paths leading to delightful little nooks among the trees where they've provided a bench or even a table and cushioned chairs where people can relax and enjoy a feeling of seclusion. I pick my way carefully down a long flight of stairs carved into the trail, avoiding the remaining muddy puddles, to the lovely natural pools and cascading waterfall. A couple of weeks ago, Ruth and I wore our swim suits down here and splashed around in the water. A lady who was content to simply dip her toes in the water while we ducked under the waterfall told us she surprised a couple skinny-dipping in the pools the day before. How embarrassing! Today is still far too cool for me to consider another swim, but just listening to the water is heavenly.

After climbing back up to the campground above, I entertain myself for a bit by watching someone back a large 5th wheel trailer into a narrow campsite while a woman with long, dark brown hair walks along beside the unit. When an older, gray-haired lady hops out of the vehicle, I smile and wave, thinking I'd like to hold up a sign above my head giving her a 10.0 score for her perfect landing. Despite having been a full-time camper for almost three years now, I still struggle with backing my little A-frame camper into a site.

"That was inspiring," I call out to her. "How did you learn to back up so well?"

She smiles. "Practice, practice, practice. There's an abandoned shopping center near my home with a huge, empty parking lot. I've spent a lot of time there working on my technique."

"I guess I need to find a place like that." I walk closer and extend my hand. "Hi. I'm Ellie."

"Virginia. Nice to meet you. And this is my daughter, Tara."

The younger woman also shakes my hand. "This is our annual mother-daughter trip. The kiddos are off with their dad for the week, so it's a perfect stay-at-home mom's vacation."

I laugh along with them. "Sounds like you have it all figured out. How many kiddos are we talking about?"

"Three boys with enough energy to power a small city for a year. Ages 4, 6, and 8."

"Whoa. No wonder you need a vacation."

Virginia chips in, pointing at herself, "Even Grandma can only handle those adorable rascals for short periods at a time. So, how about you? Any grandkids?"

I shake my head in a practiced way. "Oh, no. No children, so no grandchildren." I shrug and smile. "It just wasn't in the cards."

Virginia looks slightly embarrassed for having asked. "Oh. Well," she looks around us, "here we all are in this lovely setting." As she talks, she starts working on unhooking the trailer from her pickup. "Do you camp a lot?"

"Full time," I reply with pride.

"No kidding? That's so brave! I'm not sure I could ever sell my home and just live out of this, even though I love camping. How did you decide to take the big step?"

"Actually, a hurricane helped make the decision for me." I decide not to get into the whole mess with my husband leaving me and all that drama. "I didn't know where I really wanted to settle down, so I bought an a-frame camper on a whim and it's turned out that I still don't have a place I want to live permanently. So here I am, a full-timer."

"Wow. Very cool," she says as she heads back to her truck to pull it away from the trailer.

"What's an a-frame camper?" Tara asks.

I describe my A-Roamer and all its features to her. It's about half the length of their camper, folds down from its triangular "A" shape to a relatively low, flat box, and it feels like home to me.

"Sounds really cute. Mom and I'll come by to see it later, if that's okay."

"Absolutely. I love to show it off."

"If you don't mind my asking, isn't it hard living full time in such a small camper? You said you don't have a toilet or shower, right? And the refrigerator is really small. How do you manage?"

"To be honest," I say, scanning their spacious unit, "I'm not sure I could do it if I hadn't met my friend, Ruth, soon after I bought my trailer." I chuckle, remembering how she rescued me from my latest mini-disaster of forgetting to latch one of the triangular walls while setting it up. The wall fell over on me, and Ruth discovered me sprawled out, trying to extract myself from beneath it.

"We travel together most of the time and generally have dinner together. Her trailer isn't quite as large as yours, but it has a good-sized kitchen and fridge, so that helps a lot. As for the toilet and shower, I manage with using the ones the campgrounds provide. I don't like to impose on Ruth in that area – there can be a little too much togetherness." Although Ruth probably wouldn't mind if I showered there, I feel like she deserves a bit of private space.

"That sounds like a great friendship," Tara says.

"I'm very lucky to have her in my life," I say, blinking back sudden tears as my fears about Ruth's health rise to the surface. Fortunately, Tara's mother calls out to her to come help with something, so I seize the opening to leave. "Hey, it's been nice chatting, but I'm sure you both have things to do. I hope you'll come by later to visit. I'm in site 44."

"Will do. See you later, Ellie."

I continue my circuit through camp, eyes lowered, anxious to return to my trailer before I lose control of my emotions. What if Ruth is seriously ill? Will she move to San Diego and stay with her older daughter, Carol? Or to Wichita to be with Valerie? I can't imagine continuing to travel while she's battling cancer or whatever this might turn out to be. I feel helpless.

It's hard to imagine what would have become of me if I hadn't met Ruth when I did. I was still so uncertain about where my life was going after surviving two natural disasters plus having Franklin walk out on me. Would I have stuck with camping on my own, or settled somewhere and only taken out my A-Roamer once a year? Would I have overcome my natural shyness and made some close friends, or settled for having only a smattering of acquaintances?

Ruth is like a sister to me. Sometimes even like a mother, given our age difference. Please, please let her be okay!

"You're as jumpy as a long-tailed cat in a room full of rocking chairs," Ruth says as I drive her home from the hospital. She attempts to turn her entire body toward me so she doesn't have to twist her neck, but even out of the corner of my eye, I can see the effort is painful.

"I'm just worried about you and that spot on your x-ray," I say, reaching over to pat her knee. "And please stop trying to turn to look at me while we're in the car. I hate to see you in pain."

She inches back to a forward position. "I'm not that crazy about it, myself. But stop worrying. I'm sure I'll hear back on Monday when the radiologist or whoever looks at the new scans. There's no sense in worrying until then. The results will be the same whether we fret about them or not."

Waiting at a red light, I turn to her. "Why does it always seem like we get sick or our car breaks down just before a weekend, when you can't get anyone to do anything until they come back to work on Monday?" I huff in exasperation, then take off with a squeal of my tires as the light changes. Ruth lets out a gasp and I realize I've caused her more pain. "I'm so sorry, Ruth. I'll take it easy and not jostle you around."

"I'm fine," she says, but I can hear the stress in her voice.

When I pull into her campsite, she steers herself gently out of my SUV and walks stiffly to her camper. Charli greets her at the door as if she's been gone for months, and mews insistently, not understanding why Ruth isn't lifting her up to her favorite shoulder perch.

"How about a special toy instead, Charli?" I step back to my vehicle and empty out a small cardboard box that I've been using to hold an assortment of trail snack bars. "Here you go, little one." The cat immediately dives into the box, scrunching her rear into the almost-too-small space, and attempting to squeeze her entire body inside. If only all our problems could be solved so simply.

Ruth eases herself into her favorite cushioned chair and leans back against its pillowed headrest. "Can I get you anything?" I ask.

"How about a glass of water and one of those pills they sent home with me?"

After swallowing the pain medication, she levers the chair into a reclined position and closes her eyes. "I'm just going to take it easy for a bit. If you could set my phone here where I can reach it, I think I'll be all set. Thanks for everything you've done for me, dear."

I lean over and squeeze her hand. "You'd do the same for me. Call me if you need anything. I'll let you rest."

After moving my vehicle back to my own campsite, I decide to whip up some guacamole, which Ruth loves. Maybe after she's napped for a while, she'll want a little something to snack on. I doubt she feels up to joining some of the other campers for "happy hour" like we sometimes do after we get back from one of our hikes, but you can't always know with Ruth. She never ceases to amaze me with her energy and enthusiasm. It's hard to see her like this — so unlike her usual demeanor.

As I mash the avocado, I chuckle, recalling what Ruth and I have come to call The Guacamole Olympics. She and I were at one of those late afternoon campground gatherings with food and drinks. I had brought along a generous bowl full of my signature guacamole. Eight of us were seated around a long picnic table, pushing the bowl to one end or the other as everyone scooped tortilla chips into the yummy, green dip. Suddenly, a chipmunk leaped onto the table and made a mad dash for the bowl. Reluctant to actually strike the little animal, everyone started shouting and pounding the table and swatting at it, but the critter was not to be deterred. It scurried and dodged and faked out every palm and fist and waved twig, concluding its gymnastic performance with a perfect swan dive into the guacamole. Things happened so fast from that moment that there were eight different versions of the rest of the story, but everyone agreed that there were green blobs of dip everywhere – on the table, on people's faces and clothes, and even in one woman's long hair. We also all agreed that none of us wanted any more of that particular appetizer. The chipmunk was long gone.

There's a familiar tap at my door and I'm pleased to see that Ruth is up and about and looking like herself again. Surely someone who looks this healthy couldn't be seriously ill – could she?

"What are you doing all cooped up inside on such a beautiful afternoon?" she asks. "Let's head over to the common area for happy hour. I've got tortilla chips – any chance you could make us some of that delicious guacamole to take along?

"Funny you should ask," I say, retrieving my latest batch from the refrigerator. "Ready when you are."

Chapter 3

The next morning, Ruth is raring to take a walk. We decide to stroll around the campground and check out all the other units. Sometimes people set up elaborate displays outside their campers – especially those with large motorhomes who plan to stay in one place for an extended period of time. We admire a campsite with a huge awning hovering over an outside "room" they've created – color coordinated outdoor carpeting and lawn furniture; half a dozen potted plants; a bird feeder; sparkly gadgets that spin in the wind; wind chimes; a wooden sign hanging from a branch of a tree that reads, "The Gilford's Campsite" with an image of two people and a dog gathered around a campfire; an enormous shiny barbeque grill; and strings of lights everywhere.

When I set up camp, I toss a welcome mat in front of my steps and call it good. Ruth goes only slightly farther by including a large outdoor rug, but that's where she places her yoga mat for her morning routine.

"Surely they're full-timers," I say. Would people who still have a house to return to accumulate this much décor for camping?

"That would be my guess," Ruth says. "What do you bet

that they had a house and yard decorated to the nines before they took up camping?"

I chuckle, comparing my own home decorating with my camping style. Franklin and I kept things pretty basic. I admired my friends whose homes looked like they were straight out of an interior decorating magazine, but I never had an eye for achieving any sort of "look" other than comfortable and casual. Of course, with my miniscule camper, "décor" could quickly turn into "clutter."

Continuing along the lane, we spot a man in the distance walking toward us. As he draws closer, my initial impression is reinforced. Big, bushy white beard, rosy cheeks, eyeglasses, rather rotund – the guy would make a perfect Santa. Other than the fact that he's wearing plaid shorts that end at his knees, red suspenders, and a white tank top. And sandals.

"Good morning, ladies!" he says with a perfect ho-ho-ho sort of Santa voice.

We say *Good morning* back in chorus, both grinning like little kids. "You must get this a lot—" Ruth starts to say.

"That I look like Santa Claus?" he says, laughing. "No, hardly ever." Ho-ho-ho. "Where are you ladies from?"

We tell him our standard short versions of where we've each lived before starting the camping phase of each of our lives, and explain how we met in a campground about two years ago. "And how about you? Where are you from?" I ask.

"Surely you jest. The North Pole, of course."

Okay, so he's totally into the Santa thing. That's cool.

It's then that I realize there is a woman with her two young children standing about ten feet away from us. The little girls are probably around three and five, and I don't think it's possible that their eyes could open any wider.

"Oh, hello there young ladies," the man says, as if noticing them for the first time. "My, you look like you are having a lot of fun camping. I like your shoes. Can you make them light up again for me?"

They look at each other, then both stomp their feet rapidly to trigger the flashing LEDs in their sneakers. The older girl speaks first. "Are you Santa Claus?" Her sister nods, staring at him intently.

"How did you know my name?" he says, laughing. "Yes, I am. What are your names?"

"Celia," the five-year-old says. The smaller girl's answer is incomprehensible to my ear, but Santa seems to understand.

"Celia and Bethany! What pretty names." Then, turning to their mother, he says, "If you don't mind, may I bring something by your site for the girls in a little while?"

The children gasp in joy and jump up and down as their mother agrees.

"I'll see you later then, children," he says. He winks, then waves as he continues his walk.

That evening, we spot Celia and Bethany again as they walk past Ruth's site. The girls are clutching something in their hands, and run over to show us when we call out our hellos.

"Look it! Look it!" The little one is waving a large photo around too quickly for me to see what it is, but her sister hands hers over for our inspection. It's a photo of Santa Claus in full winter garb, autographed and personalized to Celia.

What a sweet man. I wonder if he keeps a stash of Santa photos everywhere he goes so he can give them to the children he meets.

"Maybe he really is Santa Claus," Ruth says after the family continues on their way.

"I guess we'll never know for sure," I say, wrapping an arm around her shoulder and giving it a squeeze. She hugs me back and we continue our dinner preparations with huge smiles on our faces.

***

Back at my site, my phone *pings* with a message. It's from my brother-in-law, Hank. He's sent a photo of himself and his wife, Cheryl, posing in front of the Lincoln Memorial in Washington, D.C. I reply with a shot of the lovely water feature in our campground. It's then that I realize that I never read the odd private message on Facebook that came in two days ago when Ruth had her accident. Retrieving it, I see that it is from Lisa Johnson – I don't know her. I'm about to mark it as spam, but hesitate. Could this be someone I've met camping or hiking, but never asked for her full name? I think I met a Lisa not long after I started camping – or was it Lita? I should check it out.

With an audible gasp, I read the note, my jaw hanging open.

i'm looking for eleanor driskel who lived in or near vanderwal ia in 1973. have i found the right eleanor?

Who in the world is this Lisa and why is she asking about Vanderwal? How did she find out? On Facebook, I list my name as Ellie Driskel Dwyer, following the example of some of my old college friends who include their maiden names so friends can find them in a search. Now I'm thinking that was unwise. I never considered that someone might link me to the most difficult and disturbing part of my past through social media.

Do I answer her or not? I decide to sleep on it, although the old memories this message has awakened will surely make for a restless night.

Chapter 4

Despite tossing and turning all night, I find myself staring at the ceiling of my camper at my usual wake-up time of 6:30. Coffee – I desperately need coffee! While the water heats up, I power up my phone and it greets the new day with a *ping*, announcing that I have a new private message on Facebook.

Nervously, I tap the notification – a new note from the mysterious Lisa Johnson.

> **hi again. i was probably to criptic with my other msg so i want to know if aug 13 1973 at midwest oasis means something special to u ???**

I sit down, pressing my phone against my chest. I've got to find out who this is and just how much she knows. My gut wants me to ask, "Who the hell are you and what do you want?" and demand that she tell me how she got my private information, but my inner voice insists that I remain calm and civil.

Lisa,
Your name doesn't ring a bell. Have we
met? Why are you asking about that date
and location?

I wait, holding my phone cupped close in front of me, scrolling up and re-reading her message again and again. This is insane. I do the math and realize it's been 47 years since...

Ping.

yeah u could say we met at midwest oasis
hospital but i was a newborn so i dont
actually remember any details ;)

I can barely breathe. Oh my God. Lisa is my daughter.

***

I was only fifteen when I got pregnant – barely turned sixteen by the time I gave birth. Things were so different back then. Teenage pregnancies were scandalous, embarrassing to the families, kept quiet if at all possible. I'd seldom seen an obviously-pregnant woman at that point in my life – they were to be kept hidden from young people! I remember when my 5th grade teacher, Mrs. Galloway, got pregnant. Despite the fact that she was married, she had to quit teaching once she started to show.

It was my sophomore year of high school. Tony was a few months younger than I was and about the cutest and sexiest guy I could ever imagine. He was on the swim team and I loved watching his muscular body slice through the water and how he'd shake out his long hair like a wet dog after a race. I never dreamed that such a gorgeous boy would be interested in me, a quiet girl who might be described as kind of cute, but never considered pretty. Remarkably, he started asking if he could sit with me at lunch. Soon he was walking me home from school and we'd stop at the Dolly Madison Ice Cream shop for a date. Both of us too young to drive, we often hung out in his mother's "studio" – a detached garage behind their house that had been converted to a space where his mom could pursue her hobby of sculpting clay. With his mother off to her Tuesday afternoon bowling league or her Thursday bridge club, we had plenty of privacy to "do our homework" and be sure of no interruptions. We encouraged my parents' assumption that Mrs. Caprio was always home while we were at his place. In the vernacular of the day, we eventually "went too far" and were too damn ignorant about birth control to use a method that actually works. Birth control wasn't a topic of discussion at home, nor in the sex education lessons at school, so we relied on the misinformation from our equally ignorant peers.

Still, I knew enough to realize I was "in trouble" when I missed my period. When I told Tony, the blood drained from his face and I thought he was going to pass out. The following day, he made the gallant gesture of proposing that we get married, but it didn't take us long to both admit that the prospect of playing family for real was utterly terrifying. Even more frightening to me was the prospect of giving birth. A friend's older, married sister once described her hours of agony to us, assuring us at the end of her story that the pain was quickly forgotten once they put her baby into her arms. Okay, so if it was forgotten, why did she remember it in such detail?!

What should Tony and I do? We were only fifteen, for heaven's sake! He wouldn't even be old enough to get his driver's license by the time the baby was born. When my skirts and slacks became too tight to fasten around my waist, we realized we couldn't put it off any longer. We had no choice but to tell our parents.

My mom and dad were horrified. I still shudder as I remember the humiliating meeting we had with Tony and his parents in our living room. The adults found a litany of ways to express their disappointment with us, Dad glaring at Tony with such anger that I think he would have physically attacked my boyfriend if Mr. Caprio hadn't been sitting right there. My mother demanded that we promise never to have sex again until we were eventually married to *someone* in the very distant future, and both my parents announced that I would be sent away the moment the school year ended to have the baby far from anyone who knew us, give it up for adoption, then return home with my tail between my legs. We were never to tell a soul.

For the remainder of that semester, I felt like I was in prison. I had to come directly home from school each day, dropping out of drama club and girls' choir. I never left the house evenings or weekends unless accompanied by a parent. I was forbidden from going out with Tony or even talking to him on the phone. My wardrobe transformed into baggy sweaters and loose-fitting slacks, or tent dresses, and Tony began avoiding me at school. The day after the term ended, my parents loaded me into the family car and we drove from Colorado to Iowa, where they dropped me off at my Aunt Phyllis's house. She was my dad's sister – she had never married, and I came to believe she never learned to smile. Not a day went by during my stay with her that she didn't berate me or try to humiliate me, demand that I apologize again and again for my immoral and indecent behavior.

Talk about a stereotype – pregnant teenager sent off to stay with an aunt. After a miserable summer with Aunt Phyllis in the Iowa heat and humidity, I went into labor three weeks before my expected due date, giving birth to a 5 pound, 10 ounce girl, perfectly healthy despite her early debut. One nurse lifted her up to show me, but before she could lay the baby in my arms, another nurse hissed something in her ear and they spirited my daughter away.

It's just as well. Knowing I'd never see her again, I think it would only have made things worse if I had held my baby.

Papers were signed, my parents arrived to load my sagging body and my few belongings back in the car, and home we went. As was common back then, the baby's adoption was "closed" – a secret. I didn't know who adopted her and they didn't know anything to identify me, only a smattering of my health information. Once back in Denver, I learned that Tony and his family had moved across town, he'd transferred to a different high school, and he was going steady with some other girl. I immersed myself in my school work and did my best to pretend the previous nine months happened to somebody else.

Eventually I lost the extra weight. Actually, I hadn't gained as much as the doctor would have liked while I was pregnant. By no means did she starve me, but Aunt Phyllis refused to give in to my food cravings or to allow me to "eat for two." I had no money of my own and she kept me on an extremely short leash, never letting me forget how humiliating it was to be seen in public with me, a "loose" girl, a "slut."

"You brought this all on yourself, young lady!" she declared time and time again. Back home at last, I'm sure many of my girlfriends knew the real reason I had gone away, since most avoided me once I returned. For the first several weeks of 11th grade, I was all too aware of people staring and whispering. Over time, the other kids lost interest in me and I was able to fade into the background. I was freaked out about dating anyone again, and dodged any attention from boys throughout the remainder of high school. It wasn't until I went away to college that I began to accept dates. And you'd better believe that I became well-versed in contraception before I chose to have sex again! In my early twenties, when I was involved with Franklin and he noticed my stretch marks, I claimed that they were the result of being quite fat when I was younger, then losing the weight.

Blowing out a long breath, I pick up my phone and read Lisa's note again.

I really should answer it. It's not her fault that my unwanted pregnancy was such a traumatic experience for me. I put all this behind me. I'm a grown woman now. I don't have to buy in to all the negativity of what happened almost half a century ago. I have a daughter and she wants to connect with me. She wants to know me.

The more I think about it, the more intrigued I am. What has her life been like? Do we share any interests? I realize that I haven't even looked at her online photos yet to see if she looks more like me or like Tony, so I pull up her profile to discover a pretty woman – much prettier than I ever was – with hair a similar shade of brown as mine was before I went gray. Studying her face, I suppose her smile is just a bit like mine and perhaps her eyes are like Tony's. It's been so long since I last saw him that I can't say for certain, but I remember he had dreamy, dark brown eyes.

My daughter!

She has only posted a few photos, and I can't identify her for sure in a group shot, or if she's the woman posing at a distance by a pretty lake.

Okay, enough procrastinating. I'm going to answer her.

Lisa,

I don't know how you were able to track me down, but I'm pleased that you did. I would love to get to know a bit about you. As you are probably aware, I never knew the names of the couple who adopted you, so I didn't have any way of contacting you all these years.

Would you like to talk by phone?

I include my number as well as my email address, since I find it easier to communicate longer notes that way instead of using text messaging. Should I say "*Dear* Lisa" instead of just her name? No, probably too soon for that. I debate how to wrap up my reply – do I use "Regards" or "Best wishes"? And then what? "Your mother" or "Mom" or "Ellie" or...? Then I remember Ruth's grandson telling me that it isn't necessary to sign off like I would in an old-fashioned letter. Good – I don't have to decide.

My heart pounding, I hit send.

***

After waiting for twenty minutes, but receiving no answer from Lisa, I stick my phone in my pocket and head over to Ruth's place. She looks as tired as I am.

"Good morning, dear," she says, sipping from her mug. "I overslept this morning – didn't sleep well. I hope you haven't been waiting around all this time for me to finally get up."

All this time? It's not even 7:30 yet. "I just got up, myself," I say. "I couldn't sleep either. Were you worrying about hearing from the hospital today?"

She sighs. "I wouldn't call it worrying so much as thinking through possible logistics if I need some sort of treatment. Silly of me, really. There's no sense in trying to make plans for something when I have no information to base them on."

"Any idea when they might call?"

Waving dismissively, she says, "Forecasting that is like predicting the weather a month from now. I can postulate all I like, but that's not going to change the facts." She takes a final swallow of coffee and rises from the camp chair. "Let's take a walk. I'll keep my phone handy just in case, but I doubt I'll hear anything from the doctors until at least 9 o'clock."

While she steps inside to rinse her mug, I check my phone

again to make sure I haven't missed a text or email from Lisa. Nothing yet.

***

Unwilling to drive anywhere and possibly miss a call if we're outside of the service area, we hang around camp after our walk. I'm torn between waiting near Ruth's place for the hospital to call, so I'll know right away what's going on with her lungs, or returning to my camper so I can speak with Lisa privately if she finally calls.

"You're even jumpier today than you were driving me home from the hospital," Ruth says. "Maybe you should drive into town and run some errands or something to get your mind on something other than this phone call."

For an instant, I think she's referring to the call *I'm* waiting for, but of course she knows nothing about that. "I just don't want to miss..."

Before I can finish my sentence, Ruth's cell phone rings.

"Hello, this is Ruth Erlich," she answers. "Yes, doctor."

At last! I hope he's calling with the results of her scan. I hold my breath, wishing she'd put him on speakerphone.

"I see," she says.

I can't read her expression. Is he telling her good news or bad? I mouth, "What?" and hold out my arms, shrugging with palms up, as a pantomime reinforcing the question.

"Yes."

Come on, Ruth! Give me a hint of what he's saying.

"Well, thank you very much for calling, Doctor." Pause. "Yes, I will." Another pause. "Goodbye."

Before she even has time to tap the red *end call* button on her phone, I'm pressing her for information. "What did he say?"

She gently shakes her head from side to side. "Oh, Ellie. You are too much of a worrier. Everything is fine. There's

25

nothing wrong with my lungs. We can sleep soundly tonight."

I sink onto the seat opposite her. "Oh, I'm so relieved! You can't believe how worried I was."

Her face lights up with a devilish grin. "Oh yes I can. I know you, Ellie Dwyer. You are a world class worrier. Maybe I can convince you to start doing yoga with me in the mornings. It can be quite calming, you know."

"You're back to your yoga exercises already? Doesn't your neck hurt too much?"

She shrugs. "I'm not back to my entire routine yet, but that'll come around. In fact, this might be a great time for you to give it another shot. I'll probably only do about four or five poses for the rest of this week, so it won't seem so overwhelming for you to learn. It's great for flexibility, but also for your state of mind."

"Hmm. Maybe," I say as she steps inside, returning quickly with two yoga mats.

I don't think I can finagle my way out of this.

Chapter 5

The next morning, a rap on my door is followed by Ruth calling out, "Ellie, I'm going stir-crazy. Let's go for a hike."

She steps up into my camper dressed in her typical brilliant colors – a neon-green shirt with a rainbow bouquet of flowers across the front, deep green leggings, and an orange visor. Her short-cropped white hair pokes up in little spikes atop her head. Although her posture reflects how stiff her neck must still be, she seems to be back to her usual, sunny self.

"Are you sure you're up for that?" I say, feeling the twinges in my legs as I stand. Getting out of bed this morning was an eye-opener. Yesterday's yoga lesson made me discover muscles I didn't even know I had, and every one of them is stiff.

She waves a hand at me dismissively. "Of course. Now, I was thinking of repeating that pretty walk along the river that we did a couple weeks ago. Are you up for that?"

I hesitate for a beat or two, glancing at my phone on the table. Last night, unlike my usual habit of turning it off when I go to bed, I left it on and within arm's reach, anxious to hear back from Lisa. There's still been no word from her this morning, and there's no cell service along the river trail. That's two nights in a row that I haven't slept well.

"Okay, we can do that." A gentle walk might do me good,

both physically and emotionally. I need to mellow out. If Lisa isn't one to answer messages immediately, or is reluctant to talk by phone, I don't want to overwhelm her by insisting on a conversation right away. Except she did contact *me* initially, not the other way around.

Once we're hiking, I push thoughts of my daughter aside as best I can. The river and its surroundings are even lovelier than I remembered from our previous visit. The sunlight sparkles off the water, filtering through the canopy of trees along the shore. All the sounds of traffic and people are drowned out by the splash and flow of the water, whose cascading rhythms begin to sound like a musical chorus.

When we arrive at a peaceful nook with a rustic bench carved from downed tree trunks, we sit and take out the peanut butter and banana sandwiches I put together for us.

"Still feeling okay?" I ask.

With the slightest of nods, Ruth says, "Fine. Just a bit stiff yet. But what about you? How are you doing?"

"Me? I'm okay. My legs just aren't used to all those stretches, but walking has loosened them up."

She reaches out and gives my arm an affectionate squeeze. "That's not what I meant. I know you, Ellie. There's something going on with you. Something's bothering you. Do you want to talk about it?"

At times, I think she can actually read my mind. During these past couple of years, she always seemed to know when I needed to talk about my husband, Franklin – our abrupt separation and all that happened afterwards. But this thing with Lisa – I don't know if I'm ready to tell anyone about her. She's part of a secret I've kept for my entire adult life. I never even told Franklin that I had had a baby years before he and I met.

I've lied to my husband. I've lied to my best friend. I've lied to everyone. And to think of how angry and hurt I was when Franklin hid his enormous secret – how could I have

28

been so self-righteous after all that I kept from him?

"Earth to Ellie," Ruth says, jolting me out of my memories.

"Oh. Sorry – I guess I kind of spaced out just then." I rise to my feet. "Ready to head back?"

She raises her eyebrows and looks at me skeptically. "Sure," she says, rising and rolling her shoulders slowly. "I'm good to go."

As we approach the footbridge leading back over the water, I grab her arm in alarm. "What *is* that?" I whisper urgently. Through the branches of the vegetation along the river, I caught a glimpse of something lumbering across the bridge. Something *big*.

"I don't know," she murmurs back, but then creeps forward, pulling me along with her.

"Maybe we should turn around," I say, releasing my grip on her arm. To my horror, she continues approaching the mysterious thing, which is still hard to see clearly.

A loud roar causes me to let out a high-pitched squeal before I clamp my hands over my mouth. Ruth bursts out laughing. "Come up here where you can see better," she insists.

My heart still pounding, I edge closer and stare at the "creature" cavorting on the bridge. It's someone in a dinosaur costume with the animal's head rising well over the height of the person inside the outfit. As he turns toward us, the neck and head bounce repeatedly as the tail of the ensemble wags back and forth, sweeping the surface of the walkway. It roars again and wiggles tiny front "arms" in our direction. Now that I know what I'm hearing, I can only laugh along with Ruth at how obviously fake his roar is. A young man stands on the opposite shore taking a video of the "monster," which is actually quite amusing to watch.

"Well, that's something you don't see every day," Ruth comments, wiping tears of laughter from her cheeks. She insists on posing for photos with the dinosaur man and exchanges contact information with the photographer so he'll send her copies.

The costumed man and his buddy accompany us to the parking lot where we help extract him from the outfit. We get a few more photos of him, human upper body exposed above the reptile's body, arms around both Ruth's and my shoulders. We wave goodbye to the young men as we drive out of the lot.

"If my neck weren't so stiff, I'd have asked to try on that outfit," Ruth says. "Not that I'm as old as a dinosaur, mind you. It just would have been fun."

Yep, that's my Ruth. Never too old to play like a kid.

Chapter 6

After sharing a dinner of spaghetti and meatballs with Ruth, I return to my camper for the evening, debating about sending Lisa another message in case she just never saw my last note. Was I out of line giving her my phone number and asking her to call? Have I scared her off?

"No, that doesn't make any sense," I say aloud. "She reached out to *me*."

Maybe she got cold feet after actually finding her real mother. Has she harbored feelings of anger toward me for giving her up? Perhaps she feels that a phone call might be too upsetting. She might have had some sort of emergency. Or it could be that she just doesn't feel like everything has to happen quickly – *boom, boom, boom* – like I tend to.

I call up our previous conversation and compose a new message in my head.

Hi again. Just checking that you got my last note. Give me a call.

No. That sounds like I'm nagging. How about:

> **I'd love to learn more about you. Can we
> talk by phone?**

That might scare her off even more. After a bit more consideration, I come up with something that feels more appropriate.

> **I imagine you have tons of questions for
> me. What would you like to know?**

Satisfied, I fire it off into the great unknown, or the cloud, or wherever messages go before they show up on someone else's phone.

I'm shocked when a notification pings on my phone less than a minute later. It's her!

> **sorry i didnt get bk 2 u sooner ... daughter
> emily having a little crisis haha u know how
> kids can be!!!**

Her daughter? I have a granddaughter!

> **Nothing too serious, I hope. How old is
> Emily? Do you have any other children?**

This is really happening! Not only do I have a grown daughter, I have even more of an extended family than I ever knew. Suddenly I want to know all I can about these relatives that I had banished to the remotest corner of my mind.

> **emily is almost 18 going to college this fall
> we hope
> michael is 22 just graduated & started work
> at tech startup**

I'm still dying to call and actually hear her voice. I'm not very fast at typing on my phone, so any conversation is going to lag tremendously compared to actually speaking. I need the nuance and tone of actual speech.

I'd love to talk by phone. Would it be convenient to talk now, or is there a better time?

I provide my phone number again and cross my fingers that she'll call tonight. Staring at the screen, I await her response, either to schedule a time to talk or to actually call now. A minute goes by. Two minutes. Three.

can i call u tomorrow nite? things going on i gotta take care of 2nite & i work during the week

I quickly respond with:

Absolutely. We'll talk tomorrow evening. I'm really looking forward to it!

A "Friend" request from Lisa pops up on my screen and I accept it immediately.

At least I won't be afraid to silence my phone when I go to bed tonight. I hope I'm able to sleep. Waiting to hear my daughter's voice for the first time, I know I'll be antsy overnight and all day tomorrow. Lisa must have inherited Tony's relaxed demeanor. She sure didn't get that from me.

I wonder if Lisa works or if she stayed home to raise the kids. What were her adoptive parents like? Did she have a happy upbringing? What do they think of her contacting me after all these years? Will they want to connect with me as well? I'm not sure how I feel about that prospect.

It sounds like her children have done well in school, although I wonder why she said "I hope" after telling me that Emily starts college at the end of the summer. Maybe Emily is nervous about that big step. And Michael – he must be pretty brainy to be part of a tech startup. Of course, that could also be risky and he might fall flat on his face.

What about Lisa's husband? She didn't include his name on her Facebook profile, but that doesn't necessarily mean anything. There's a photo on her page of a group of young people who seem to be in their late teens or early twenties. Are her children in this shot? I search for a resemblance to Lisa's picture, but don't come to any conclusion.

The questions keep multiplying and I can tell it'll be very difficult to turn off my brain and get some sleep tonight. This may be one of those nights when I give up on trying and just get up and read until I finally nod off. Something light and funny. I'll look through my to-be-read list and come up with something other than the complex murder mystery I started yesterday.

Chapter 7

It's moving day – the first of two moves I need to make to a different site within this same campground. I figure I won't have to be as compulsive as usual about putting everything away, since I'm only towing the camper a few hundred yards and plan not to exceed five miles per hour. Still, I go through my printed checklist to make sure I'm not forgetting something important, like raising the stabilizer legs so they don't drag along the ground, likely destroying their crank mechanisms as well as tearing nasty gouges in the pavement. I'd be unhappy and the campground owners would probably ban me for life.

I fold down the triangular sides of the a-frame, then drop the big end walls into place. As often happens, a couple walking past as I work stops to watch the transformation from pointy little house to flat box.

"That is so cute," the woman says. "I always wondered how those things fold down. Is it hard to put back up again?"

"Not too bad," I reply as I consider latching the roof in place. Do I really need to for such a short trip? Yeah, I probably should – better safe than sorry.

"If you really want to see how it works, just follow me over to site 103 and you can watch." Their faces light up as they nod to each other. We camper folks are easily entertained.

I finish my final checklist and hop into my Jeep. Just as I'm about to start the engine, I hear a familiar voice call out.

"Ellie? What's going on?" Ruth walks up beside the driver's side window, Charli sprawled around her neck. "You're leaving?" I've never before heard her sound so hurt and confused.

"No, of course not! Remember? They weren't able to change around the next reservation for this site when we asked for an extension, so I have to move to a vacant spot."

She looks baffled. Oh, dear. Could she be having memory issues since the accident?

"Oh. How foolish of me to think you would just up and leave." She frowns in concentration. "But I sure don't remember your telling me you'd have to change sites. I'm sorry to be the cause of all this bother for you."

Still concerned about her memory, I paste on a broad smile. "It's hardly any bother at all, Ruth – don't think of it like that. I'd rather stay on here and continue doing things together than move on to Crater Lake without you."

"All right, then. What is your new site number? Charli and I will come on over and help you get settled in again."

So now I have a small parade of people following me along the campground road to help install me in my new location. Worried that the walkers might feel like they need to rush, I try to keep my speed down to their pace. As I creep along, other people in their campsites watch with curious faces. "What's going on?" one man calls out to my ensemble.

"Just helping my friend Ellie move to another loop," Ruth replies.

"Is that one of those hard-shelled pop-ups?" he asks.

The woman following me explains that she and her husband want to see it being put back up and the new man joins us. I can't really see the line of folks behind me in my mirrors – only Ruth, who is walking right along the left edge of the road. But I can hear their enthusiastic voices.

By the time I pull into site 103, it seems like my ultra-short trip has become the social event of the lunch hour. Thank goodness I don't have to back into my new space in front of a large audience – the driveway is a long, curved, pull-through. Hopping out of my SUV, I'm startled to discover that my followers have grown to seven people. They are happily mingling about, enjoying conversations with newly-introduced friends and fussing over the cat.

"It's show time," I announce once I've leveled and unhitched the trailer from the car. I appoint one of the men to stand opposite me to help lift the camper walls and he grins like a little boy at being the one chosen. Within thirty seconds, the walls are all in place and latched and the show is over. "Thanks for coming, everyone. Please excuse us while I finish getting things put away inside. It's been nice meeting all of you."

I said "us" instead of "me" so Ruth could take a break. Although the cat is quite petite, her insistence on being toted around today was probably hard on Ruth's neck. Now that she realizes she's being separated from her new fan club, Charli bounds outside again to mingle with the people who are still hanging around, swapping travel stories.

***

Once I'm settled, I offer to make lunch for us. My mind leaps from anticipation of talking to my daughter tonight on the phone to concern about Ruth's earlier lapse in memory. I place the sandwiches, sliced apple, and cups of water on the table and sit down, noting that Ruth is staring into my face with an odd expression on hers.

"Thanks for the lunch," she says, but doesn't pick up her

sandwich. "Ellie, there's something I've been wanting to talk to you about."

I finish chewing my first bite and set my food back on the plate. "Okay. I'm listening."

"I'm concerned about you, dear. You've seemed quite preoccupied recently, and even a bit forgetful."

What? *I'm* forgetful?

She continues, "Something is clearly on your mind. I'll tell you about an email I received from my grandson, Gabe, and later you don't seem to remember anything about it. Or this business of moving to a different campsite. I suppose you believe you told me about it, but I'm quite sure you only let me know that we could stay on here for another eight days."

I start to open my mouth to correct her, but it dawns on me that she may be right. I don't actually recall telling her all the details of our new arrangement. It's quite possible that her memory is perfectly fine – it's mine that's in question.

"Maybe it will help to get it off your chest. What's bothering you, dear?"

In that moment, I realize how crazy it is that I'm still keeping this secret from the world. Here I am, hoping to form some sort of link to this grown woman, Lisa, who is my biological child, and I'm simultaneously trying to keep anyone from knowing I had a baby when I was sixteen? How could I possibly manage to keep this from Ruth, even if I wanted to?

Wasn't there a famous quote, "The truth shall set you free"? Okay, then. Here goes.

"I've been keeping a secret almost all my life and I've just realized it's time for me to stop lying." My throat feels tight and I find it hard to look Ruth in the eye. She reaches across the table and takes my hand in hers and I take a bracing breath. "I told you I didn't have any children, but that's not true. I have a daughter. I got pregnant when I was quite young and gave her up for adoption, so we've never met."

"Oh, Ellie. Did you imagine I'd think less of you if I had known? That's not the case at all. These things happen. That doesn't make you a bad person."

I wipe my hands across my face, realizing that I have started to cry. She comes around the table and sits beside me, rubbing my back in circles to comfort me. I sniff and try to regain control of my emotions. "So, the incredible thing is that my daughter has contacted me. We've exchanged a few messages through Facebook."

Hearing the happiness in my voice, Ruth gives me a hug. "Wow. That's marvelous. Now, how does it feel to get that out in the open, dear?"

Wiping my eyes and beaming, I nod. "It feels really damn good. You can't imagine how much shame and embarrassment I've carried all these years. My family didn't exactly greet the news with warmth and understanding."

I tell her about being sent off to live with Aunt Phyllis in Iowa and her constant ostracizing. She made me feel humiliated about ever appearing in public, saying I should be ashamed to let anyone see my body, which was flaunting my sinful behavior to everyone around me. Although giving up the baby for adoption felt like a huge relief, I wonder how much that experience changed my whole outlook on having children.

Three years into our marriage, Franklin was the one to raise the topic of starting a family. I felt ambiguous about the prospect, but feigned enthusiasm. We actually did try to get pregnant – for a couple of months, anyway. After that, I'm ashamed to admit, I secretly went back on the pill. As time passed, my husband broached the subject of asking for medical advice. Reminding him of my sometimes irregular periods and occasional over-the-top PMS, I suggested that I be the one to be checked first. Instead of asking my gynecologist about becoming pregnant, we reviewed contraceptive choices and she prescribed a different version of the pill. I reported back to Franklin that it was extremely unlikely that I could become pregnant and admitted that I was able to accept that. "I guess it just wasn't meant to be," I told him, suggesting we focus on other children in our lives, like his brother's two kids and the offspring of some of our friends. Clearly disappointed, he offered gentle suggestions about seeking other opinions or pursuing alternatives such as adoption, but I nudged each idea aside.

Why didn't I want to have a child once I was in a stable marriage with the resources to raise and support one? I suppose it was a product of vividly imagining myself as a mother back when I was pregnant with Lisa. The prospect was terrifying at the time, but even after her birth and adoption, I often revisited the idea in my head, trying to picture myself married and capable of taking on such responsibility. Even as my perspective changed, I couldn't envision myself in the role of a "good mother." I enjoyed my writing job and everything about our lifestyle, and the desire to be a parent just wasn't there. Ever.

When I hit forty, I had my tubes tied, convincing Franklin that a surprise pregnancy at that age would be risky, both to myself and to a baby. "Wouldn't it be just our luck," I said, "to get pregnant when we're no longer wanting that?" By then, even he was pretty locked into the flexibility and freedom that being childless offers.

"If Franklin were still around," I say to Ruth, "I would finally tell him about my daughter. I'm ashamed of how I deceived him. And you."

"Deceived me? I can't imagine how," she says.

"By telling you I didn't have kids. I probably even claimed it was a big disappointment for my husband and me."

"Oh, Ellie. You're much too hard on yourself. You don't owe everyone in the world a detailed explanation of your life history. Saying that you didn't have kids is fine. Frankly, asking a new acquaintance if they have children can sometimes be too personal a question, in my experience. Or how many they have. What if they've lost a child? Sometimes it's best to just give the short, simple answer rather than get into all the details."

"I suppose." I lean over and plant a kiss on her cheek. "How did you get to be so wise, Ruth?"

She doesn't answer right away and I realize she is lost in thought, a frown on her face.

"Ruth? Is everything okay? Are you in pain?"

She sighs deeply. "I'm not wise. I've just had a lot of life experiences in my eighty-two years. Here's another thing you and I have in common – upsetting pregnancies that we seldom talk about."

She's never mentioned any problems when she was carrying either of her daughters, but maybe there were complications with one or both of them. I wait to see if she'll say anything further.

"Of course, you know my daughters Carol and Valerie."

I nod. I've only met Valerie once, briefly. She's the quiet, serious one. But Carol and her husband Nick have joined us twice at National Parks and we spent a week together each time. She clearly takes after her mother, outgoing and adventurous.

Ruth sighs. "What I rarely tell anyone is that I became pregnant again when I was 42. The girls were 12 and 16 by then. We were all surprised by the news, of course, but very excited as well. By then, doctors were routinely using ultrasound, so we knew we were having a boy." She pauses, staring into the distance. "We decided we'd name him Joshua. Joshua David Erlich."

"David, after his father," I say.

She nods. "We didn't want him to be a *junior* or *David II*. So we made that his middle name. Anyway," she continues with a slight tremble to her voice, "the rest of the news from the first ultrasound wasn't so good. He wasn't developing like he should. But we were optimistic and also extremely naïve. We held family conferences and all agreed that we would still love Joshua even if he had disabilities. But as the weeks and months went by, the doctors became more and more concerned about his condition. And we grew more and more determined that we could offer this baby a loving home, no matter what."

A tear rolls down her cheek. "I was 30 weeks into the pregnancy – about 7 months – when the information from the doctors finally began to sink in. The baby was unlikely to live much longer inside of me, but if by some miracle he managed to survive until birth, he wasn't expected to live more than an hour or so, and that would be with major medical intervention. His brain had barely developed and he had serious issues with his heart, his lungs ... pretty much everything. And the latest blow was that continuing the pregnancy was becoming more and more risky for my own health. They urged me to let them terminate the pregnancy before it ended up killing me."

"Oh my God, Ruth. I had no idea." Tears are leaking from my eyes, but I ignore them.

Rubbing her hands together, she fixes her gaze on them. "My husband and daughters finally convinced me to have the abortion. They were devastated at the thought of not having that baby brother, but were determined not to lose me as well." She sniffs loudly and digs a tissue from her pocket. "I could hardly get out of bed for the next three months. Not because of physical issues – I was just so depressed over it all. But David helped me come back, reminding me how much the girls – and he – still needed me." She clears her throat and sits up tall. "It was the hardest period of my life, but our family eventually came out the other side stronger and closer than ever."

"I feel like a fool," I say, "making such a fuss over being embarrassed as a teenager. That was nothing compared to what you've been through."

She rises and waves her hands at me, signaling me to

stand. We throw our arms around each other and rock gently for several minutes, each lost in our own thoughts. We're interrupted by an insistent meowing outside my camper door.

"Did you think we'd forgotten you, Charli?" Ruth says as we open the door and the cat rushes inside, still vocalizing loudly.

"I'll bet she'd like some of that sliced turkey. Is it okay if I give her some?" I ask.

Ruth smiles and her warmth and love shine from her eyes. "Sure, but just be forewarned. One time she got so excited about smoked turkey breast that she actually peed herself."

"No! Really?"

She nods. "Thankfully, she was perched on a vinyl kitchen chair at the time, so it wasn't as bad as it could have been. Now, she was still pretty much a kitten at the time, and she hasn't done anything like that since, but you might want to feed her outside."

I follow her advice. As Charli devours the meat, Ruth wraps her arm around my waist. "So, what's happening next with your daughter? Have you two made any plans to meet?"

With my arm around her shoulder, I say, "We're taking things slowly – kind of like going on a blind date. She's supposed to call tonight after she gets off work, so this'll be our first actual spoken conversation."

"I'm happy for you, dear. It's obvious that this means a lot to you. Let me know how your big date goes."

I smirk. "Okay, *Mom*."

She wags a finger at me. "And don't you stay up past your curfew, you hear?" she says, trying to keep a straight face. We giggle like a couple of young girls as we stroll back to her end of the campground, Charli following close behind in case I might produce some more turkey breast.

Chapter 8

My hand trembles in anticipation as I answer a call from an unfamiliar number.

"Hi, it's me. Your daughter, Lisa."

Blinking back tears, I answer, "I'm so happy to hear your voice. And I know I told you this already, but thank you for searching for me and reaching out."

"No problem. I've wondered about you all my life, but it wasn't until one of my friends started researching her family tree that I thought I might really be able to find you."

"That must have been quite some detective work. I thought your adoption records were sealed."

"Oh, yeah. Well, since I'm an adult and I'm the one who was adopted, I found out there was a way for me to get your name. And my parents knew what hospital I was born in, so I took it from there. Anyway, I've got like a million questions for you, if that's okay." She laughs. "Well, not really a million, so don't panic or nothin'."

As a professional proofreader, I could be someone who insists on pointing out bad grammar, but that's not the sort of person I am. Although I just corrected her in my mind, I'd never dream of saying anything out loud. "I'm not panicking," I say in a playful tone. "Where do you want to begin?"

"That's cool. So, do you have any kids? Besides me, I mean."

"No, I never had any more children. I was married for almost forty years, and we tried to get pregnant, but ..." I pause, torn between telling her the truth or brushing it aside, as I've always done.

"But?"

Would she feel better or worse if I admit that I didn't want children? Am I ready to start telling the truth now that I've confided in Ruth? I take a bracing breath. Even now, it's not easy to think about Franklin. "Uh, it just didn't work out." Maybe I'll tell her more once we get to know each other better.

"Oh. Sorry," she says, but quickly continues. "I'm divorced. Raised my two kids pretty much on my own. He was a deadbeat dad – never paid support. Anyways, we managed okay. My parents – well, you know, the folks who adopted me – they left us a little bit of money after they died in a car crash a while back. I mean, we went through it kinda quick, but at least it got Michael through college. There ain't much of anything left now, though, for Emily, so that's kind of a bummer."

Her parents both died in an accident? "I'm so sorry to hear that, Lisa. That must have been awfully hard on all of you to lose your parents. Do you have other family around – aunts, uncles, cousins?"

There's a pause before she answers. "Nope. Nobody like that. 'Least not that I ever got to meet. But don't worry. Me and the kids got through it okay. I been working two jobs since my divorce and Michael, he always got work shovelin' snow in the winter and mowin' lawns in the summers. Emily, she's been flippin' burgers after school. Hard workers, both of 'em. Got good grades in school, too. I'm real proud of my kids."

"It sounds like there are plenty of reasons to feel proud. You've obviously raised them well."

"Thanks. I tried, anyhow. Say," she says in an upbeat voice, "they're your grandkids, ain't they? I just realized that!"

My face feels like it could crack wide open, I'm smiling so broadly. "Yeah. I guess they are. How about that?"

"Yeah. How about that? So, listen, um ... Ellie. Should I call you that? Or would it be alright if I call you *Mom*? I always called my, uh, other mother *Mama*, so I'd like to save that name just for her, you know?"

The lump in my throat feels like it will be impossible to speak, but I manage to choke out the words. "I'm touched and honored that you want to call me Mom. Thank you, Lisa. I can't begin to tell you how much that means to me." I grab a tissue and wipe my nose.

"Me, too. So, Mom, I'm afraid I'm going to have to go. Emily just got home from the burger joint and we got some student loan applications and stuff to fill out that needs to get in the mail tomorrow."

I could talk for another few hours, but I swallow my disappointment. "I understand. Let's talk again soon," I say, picking up a pen from a small box of odds and ends that I keep on the counter. "When would be good for you? My time is completely open, so it's entirely up to you."

She doesn't answer right away. "Okay, so things are pretty crazy around here, but how about I call again on Sunday afternoon?"

I had hoped for tomorrow, but remind myself that I went 47 years without contact with my daughter, so surely it won't be that difficult to wait three days to talk again. I can always send her a text in the meantime. "Sounds great. Talk to you then, Lisa."

"Cool. Later, Mom." She ends the call.

Mom. I'm beaming with joy. Pretty darn good "blind date" if you ask me! I consider walking over to Ruth's camper to tell her all about our conversation, but realize it's almost 9:30.

She's probably already tucked into bed, reading for a while before going to sleep. It can wait until morning.

Before retiring, I log into Facebook and post several photos of the dinosaur guy and ourselves from the other day, captioning them with "A paleontologist's dream come true in Oregon." I check Lisa's page, but she hasn't posted anything new since she first contacted me. Probably too busy working and dealing with Emily's college funding to spend much time on social media.

Rats. I wanted to answer any questions she had about why I gave her up for adoption. And I forgot to ask her where she lives or what kind of work she does. Or what interests she and *my grandchildren* have.

I'm a grandma. Wow – that simple sentence carries such an astounding emotional impact. To my great astonishment, I find myself wondering how I can spoil my grandkids! Who cares if they're pretty much adults – I need to make up for lost time. Especially since they lost two grandparents so tragically. There's so much I want to know about this family that I never thought I'd want to connect with.

Although it's kind of late, I know I'm not going to be able to go to sleep while I'm so amped up. I pull on my sneakers and grab a headlamp – I'm going for a walk around the campground to burn off some of this adrenaline.

Chapter 9

It's barely 7:00 in the morning, but I'm not surprised to see Ruth doing her daily stretches on her neon-orange yoga mat, strategically placed in a patch of sunlight near her camper. I hardly slept last night, but couldn't wait to tell her about my conversation with Lisa. As I approach, Ruth unfolds and refolds her body into a new pose, then backs off to slowly stretch her neck from side to side before resuming the position.

"Your neck still hurts?" I say once I'm standing within talking distance.

She exhales slowly before speaking. "Not bad. It gets better every day." Another deep breath in, and she extends an arm higher in the air. "Two more minutes and I'll be done." Breathe out. "I want to hear about your blind date." Breathe in. "Sorry I didn't wait for you to join me."

"No problem – I'm still sore from last time."

I spot Charli sprawled out in another sunny spot and entice her to play by waving a long, skinny twig I find on the ground. We entertain ourselves as Ruth finishes her routine.

"All right, then," she says, rolling up her mat. "Tell me everything."

I repeat the entire conversation, virtually word for word. By the time I finish, there are tears in both our eyes. "I can't believe how excited I am about connecting with them. I've gone for years without giving my daughter a moment's thought, and now look at me!"

"Grandma Ellie."

I nod, grinning like a fool. "I know! Me, a grandmother! All these years I've listened to people rave about their grandchildren and carry on about what a joy and blessing they are, but I never really 'got it.' This is crazy, I know, but I think I finally understand. Even though I've never met them and I don't even know what they look like."

"Well, you'll need to rectify that right away. One of the top ten rules about being a grandma is to have photos on hand at all times so you can show off your kiddos to everyone you meet."

I laugh. "I don't recall you doing that. However, I *have* seen you pass around your phone to show off a certain little green-eyed beauty with pointy ears."

She scoops up the cat and nuzzles her soft fur. "Who, me? Fuss about little, ol' Charli?"

"Anyway, I'm on cloud nine and barely slept last night, but I need a distraction so I don't obsess all day about everything I want to talk to Lisa about next time. Any ideas?"

She gets that cheeky grin on her face that I've come to recognize as the precursor to some outrageous suggestion. Most of which haven't seemed so outrageous once she convinced me to try something new. Like kayaking. Climbing a peak that included ladders and metal walkways on the steep sections. Snorkeling. Riding an electric bike.

"Have you ever smoked marijuana?" she asks, beaming as if she is already high.

Okay, now she's outdone herself. "Never," I say. "Have *you*?" I ask, already suspecting what her answer will be.

"Oh, yes. Back in the late 70s when the girls were in college, Carol brought home a roach over Christmas break and smoked it with David and me."

I stare at her, wide-eyed. "You're kidding. You smoked dope with your daughter?"

She laughs. "With my adventurous one, yes. Now I'm sure Valerie never tried it – she's always been the straight arrow in the family. Heaven knows where she got that from! But Carol takes after me – ready to consider almost anything and she loves corrupting her own mother."

"But it was illegal back then."

She sighs and rolls her eyes. "Oh, Ellie. It sounds like you were willing to break some rules back when you were a teenager. Did that experience change you so much that you never tried doing anything again that you weren't supposed to? I suppose you never drank any alcohol in college because you were underage."

"Well ... a couple of times, actually," I say, feeling slightly guilty for having been so by-the-rules after the pregnancy. I had allowed myself a few sips of beer at one gathering; a tiny glass of overly-sweet, cheap wine at another. "Oh, wait – I almost forgot this. I did accidentally eat a brownie baked with marijuana once at a party in college. Everyone else seemed to know they were 'funny brownies' but I was clueless. It was a good thing that my girlfriend was there to tell me why I felt so strange. Once I relaxed and stopped freaking out about what I had eaten, it all seemed really funny. But I never tried it again after that."

"So, how about we go check out a marijuana dispensary? You do know it's legal here, right?" she asks, her face lit up like a little girl asking about going to a candy store.

Oh, Ruth. She never ceases to amaze me. I know she'll keep working on me until I agree, so I decide to get it over with quickly. "Okay. Since it's legal, I guess we can go take a look. But I don't have to buy anything, do I?"

She actually does a fist pump. "Great! And no, I'm not going to force you to buy something, but I might. I definitely might."

That's what I was afraid of. I know where this is going next. Well, I wanted something to distract me from obsessing about Lisa all day. This certainly will.

***

"Look – they still sell Maui Wowie!" Ruth exclaims as we peruse the display cases at Tangled up in Green, a dispensary marked with a distinctive green cross flag waving outside its door. "That was quite popular way back when Carol was in college."

"I think you'll find this to be a great deal more potent than back in those days," the young woman waiting on us explains. I eye a bumper sticker displayed on the wall – "Not your grandma's weed" – and groan softly. "Are you looking for something to toke or an edible? We have cookies and gummies. We also have edible oils and beverages, if you'd rather not smoke."

"Beverages?" Ruth asks.

"Yeah, like ginger beer and lemonade. Now, if it's been a long time since you've used pot, you might want to go with the ginger beer. It's less potent than our lemonade. We actually have two different kinds. Are you looking for a really mellow high or more of a creative high?"

Ruth looks at me. "What do you think, Ellie. Mellow or creative?"

I just shake my head. "I'll leave that up to you. I'm not planning on trying it either way."

She grins and waves off my remark. "Let's go with mellow. Is that also helpful for pain, like for a stiff neck?"

The girl nods. "So, everybody's different and we can't always predict how a product will work for everyone, but lots of people find this will help with pain, especially if it's not too severe."

"I think we'll go with the mellow ginger beer, then. And maybe your smallest package of gummies. Do they come in cherry flavor?"

I'm feeling a bit odd just breathing the unusual smells in here. Can you get high just from visiting a marijuana shop? "Ruth," I say quietly, tapping her shoulder, "I'll wait for you in the car."

She joins me several minutes later, carrying a small box that appears to have been hermitically sealed. "Okay. We're good to go!" she declares, storing her package behind the passenger seat. "Do you feel like going out to eat, or should we head back home for lunch?"

The longer we stay away from our campground, the longer I can delay her inevitable request that I try some of her goodies with her. "Let's eat out. How about that sushi place we saw on the main drag? The one with all the positive reviews?"

"Sounds perfect. Let's do it."

***

After lunch, a stroll in the town park, a visit to a row of antique stores (I've owned many of the items on display!), and grocery shopping, we head back to camp. Ruth unwraps the cannabis package and I'm relieved to see that she opted out of buying the candies and has brought back only the two bottles of magical ginger beer. "We'll have these with dinner," she declares. I cringe.

Back at my trailer, I put together a humongous salad while Ruth fires up her grill for the chicken. When I arrive at her site, she's just pulling a tray of brownies from the oven. "In case we have the munchies later," she says. "And if there are any left over, we can take them to tonight's campfire gathering." Seeing the expression on my face, she adds, "Don't worry. They're just normal brownies. No secret ingredients."

Ah, yes. The Wednesday night event where everyone is invited to come sit around a communal fire to shoot the breeze, tell some tall tales, roast marshmallows for s'mores, and try to keep the children who are totally jazzed up with sugar highs from playing tag too close to the flames. I joined the "fun" briefly the first week we were here, but it was a bit too chaotic for me. Ruth, however, hasn't missed a single time.

It's barely past 5 o'clock, but Ruth insists that we imbibe early in the evening so we can really enjoy the effects before hitting the sack. "Ready?" she says as she opens both bottles.

"I'm still not sure about this," I say, staring at the beverage in my hand. "Maybe I should just hold off and watch over you in case something goes wrong."

"Now, Ellie, where's your sense of adventure? This isn't like the old days when we really weren't sure what we were ingesting. These shops are highly regulated. We'll be fine. It's going to be fun – trust me!"

"I do trust you, but you've never drunk one of these things before, have you? How do you know what'll happen?"

She offers a Mona Lisa smirk. "I don't. That's the fun of it. Come on, Ellie. Try it – you'll like it." With that, she takes a long pull on her soda. "Hmm. Not bad. Now you."

I sigh, but comply by swallowing one gulp. Since I've never even tasted regular ginger beer before, I'm not sure what I think of the flavor. It's not bad. A little like ginger ale, but sharper, hardly sweet at all. I'll just have another sip or possibly two, then beg off from downing the rest.

She slices the grilled chicken into thin strips and divides them between the two large bowls of lettuce, red peppers, cucumbers, grape tomatoes, and shredded carrots. We perch at the picnic table and dive into our meal.

"This may sound premature, but I'm actually considering sending Lisa some money to help my granddaughter with her college expenses."

"Really? How much does she need?"

"Honestly, I don't know. But I do know she's applying for a student loan and those can be crippling to pay back. And tuition these days can be totally out of sight. Still, I figure even a little bit would help. I'm thinking maybe five hundred dollars."

A few years ago, when Franklin left me, I would have been hard-pressed to pull five hundred dollars from my savings. Now, however, my financial situation has improved and feels reasonably secure.

"Oh, my. You are definitely taking your grandmother role seriously. I'm not saying it's a bad idea, dear. Just don't get sucked into the idea that you need to make up for the years those kids were growing up. They had other family all this time."

I take another bite of salad and wash it down with ginger beer. "I know. But their maternal grandparents are gone and I get the impression that their father and his parents are totally out of the picture, so that leaves me. But I hear what you're saying. I'm not going to do anything right away."

We munch on our meal for a minute before Ruth asks, "Are you feeling anything yet?"

"Feeling...? Oh. The marijuana." I consider that a moment, looking around the campsite to see if anything looks different or feels different. "No, I don't think so. How about you?"

"Maybe a little."

I notice that she's finished her drink already, while I still have a little bit left of mine. Oh. I was going to only take a couple of sips. Oops. What the heck. I chug the rest of it down.

"I'll bet you feel it a little because *you* are so little," I say, chuckling. "They should weigh every customer and sell them different size portions. You'd get a teeny, tiny bottle of ginger beer and I'd get a medium bottle. Or when we first met, I'd have needed a large bottle." This feels very clever to me and I'm wondering why the marijuana dispensaries haven't already implemented this.

She laughs. "I think *you* are feeling it a little. Hey, are you ready for some brownies?"

"Sounds great!"

We have the wherewithal to clear the table and rinse our dishes before diving into the batch of still-warm brownies. Charli, who enjoyed a small helping of chicken while we ate, shows no interest in the chocolate treats and curls up in the middle of the picnic table to watch the world go by. We sit close to her. When she spots a bird high in a tree beside the campsite, her mouth trembles with excitement and she utters a staccato of *meh-meh-meh* sounds. Ruth and I collapse on the tabletop with giggles.

"Oh! We need to take brownies to the get-together!" she declares, so we fetch some plastic wrap and, with great difficulty and considerable mirth, manage to cover the dessert.

Walking along the campground road, we're distracted by the wonder of our long shadows stretching before us. "Look how tall you are, Ruth!" Charli bounds along the path in front of us, then stops to look back to see if we're following.

"I remember once when I was in college," I say as we pause to watch a squirrel scolding us from high in a tree, "I was walking across campus with two girls from my dorm who were both totally stoned. While I was perfectly straight, as we used to say."

"Of course you were," she says, and we both break out in giggles.

"They had some papers they needed an instructor to sign because they wanted to drop out of her synchronized swimming class." I pause, mesmerized by watching Charli slink toward the tree holding the noisy squirrel.

"So, what about the stoned girls from the dorm?" Ruth prompts.

"Oh. Right." I think a moment to gather my thoughts. "Okay. Anyway, they had these papers for her to sign and they were trying to fill them out as we walked. For the swim instructor's name, they insisted on writing 'Miss Fish' and they'd laugh hysterically as they wrote that down on both of their forms. I kept trying to get them to write her real name, but they insisted on leaving it as Miss Fish."

We laugh hysterically.

"So what happened when their teacher saw that?" she asks.

"Nothing! The swimming teacher really was named Miss Fish!" I say, and we stagger over to the nearest picnic table before we collapse with laughter.

"Uh, hello ladies." A man's voice presses through our hilarity. We're in his campsite, giggling like a couple of toddlers at his picnic table.

Ruth manages to recover first. "Oh, hi. Sorry about the noise. We were just leaving."

Which also seems incredibly funny. We jump to our feet and I manage to knock over a water bottle that was on the table. Instead of getting upset with our strange invasion of his space, the guy starts laughing along with us. And then his wife comes to the door of their RV and she joins in. A girl walking her three itsy, bitsy dogs passes by, and soon she can't help but laugh as well. The little dogs start yapping and jumping around with excitement, and more people keep getting drawn into our circle of mirth, like a black hole sucking everything into a singularity of hilarity.

"I think I may have just peed myself," I whisper into Ruth's ear, and we somehow escape the universe of merriment, leaving the brownies behind as a sacrifice to the glee gods.

"I thought that girl sold us something that would make us feel mellow," I say as we settle ourselves on the couch in Ruth's camper. I stare at the clock over her stove, trying to understand how four hours have gone past. "This seems more like silly than mellow."

She snuggles into a cushion like a cat circling to find the perfect position. "It feels like I'm transitioning to the mellow part now."

"I wonder if the gummies would have had a different effect. But, you know, I don't think I'll want to do this again anytime soon. It's been fun, but kind of ... crazy and out of control-ish. You know?"

"That's kind of the idea. But don't worry. I decided not to buy the gummies after all, so we're totally out of recreational drugs at the moment."

Hugging a pillow to my chest, I gaze at its swirling design and brilliant colors. I could stare at this for hours. "Okay. That's cool."

We both feel like our skeletons have turned into gelatinous gummies when we declare it's time to go to bed. Too relaxed to consider walking all the way back to my campsite, we opt for a slumber party of two, both falling fast asleep moments after we lie side-by-side in Ruth's queen sized bed.

Chapter 10

Pleased to discover that our recreational high hasn't left either of us with any lingering symptoms, like hangovers or uncontrollable giggling fits, Ruth and I are up early. She insists on treating me to a scrambled egg breakfast, but then I excuse myself and head back to my own place. Today is another moving day for me and my trailer, but this time I'm only shifting four sites to the south. The unfortunate news is that site 99 is a back-in, so I'll have to manage to manipulate my A-Roamer into a wide slot in reverse.

Meanwhile, the current occupants of 99 haven't departed yet, so I decide to buckle down and complete the tedious proofreading job I've been avoiding this past week. Most of the contracting gigs I take on are actually quite enjoyable and often entertaining. This one, unfortunately, has been a beast. The author seems to have been torn between composing a science fiction novel and writing a technical treatise on astrophysics. I lost track of the storyline in the third chapter and have given up on distinguishing the science jargon that is real versus what the writer has invented. And don't get me started on dealing with **All The Capital Words** that shouldn't be and the apostrophes that crop up in most, but not all, plural words. Or **Word's**, as he's typed twice in the last few paragraphs.

I work straight through until the task is finished. It takes me a full minute to unbend my back and stand tall. "One o'clock already?" I say, peering out a window toward my new locale. It's empty and beckoning.

It seems like too much bother to fold down the camper just to move it fifty yards. I gather up any loose odds and ends that might jiggle off a table and set them in the sink, detach the trailer from the electric box and the water connector, and hop into my Jeep. I maneuver the car so I'm directly in front of my trailer, then use its back-up camera to ease into position to hitch up. Although this technique usually works pretty well, there's something about the sunlight and shadows that is making it hard to be sure I'm lining up trailer ball A with trailer coupler B.

I hop out of the car and go back to take a look. Okay. A little to the right and back about two inches. I climb into the driver's seat, turn the wheel, and inch backwards. Stride back and take another close look. Hmm. Maybe just a hair forward now. I heave myself into the cab of the car again for the adjustment. Traipse back to the hitch and check. Looks about right, so I lower the jack to place the coupler onto the ball. Except it isn't going down.

"Oh no!" I forgot to raise the leveling legs on the trailer, so they're bearing all the weight instead of the jack. I quickly use the jack to alleviate the problem, take care of all the leveling legs, and pull out my checklist to see if there's anything else critical that I've forgotten.

Finally, I've got the car and the trailer hooked together and I'm ready to drive five seconds to my new campsite. Now for the part I'm expecting to be troublesome – backing into site 99. You'd think I'd be better at this after all this time, but actually I haven't had that much practice. I opt for pull-through sites whenever possible, and I don't move to a new campground more than an average of once a month.

Reviewing the process in my mind, I pull past the site to the position I think I'll need to start the backup process. Stumble out of the seat again and get a look at the big picture. Remarkably, I think I'm in a good starting spot. I trudge back up front and drag myself into the seat. I've just visualized the sequence and started to turn the wheel when a man comes up beside me.

"Hi there, young lady," he says. "Would you like me to do that for you?"

I cringe at him calling me "young lady." First off, I think I'm likely a bit older than he is, so it comes off as totally fake. Second, his whole tone and manner is condescending, not at all like someone who is simply offering assistance if needed.

I give him my sweetest smile. "No, thank you. But there is one thing you could do for me, if you don't mind my asking."

His grin turns to a leer and his tone changes. "At your service, young lady. What can I do for you, gorgeous?" He wiggles his eyebrows suggestively, hooks his thumbs in his pants pockets, fingers outlining his crotch, and thrusts his hips forward.

Ruth would probably hop out and physically confront him – all five foot, one inch of her. In an earlier version of myself, I would have smiled uncomfortably and possibly even let him back up my camper for me. But not today.

"You could go back to your own campsite and never bother me again," I say, channeling my inner "Go ahead, make my day" growl a la Clint Eastwood. He steps back from my Jeep, a look of complete astonishment on his face.

"What the hell did *I* do?" he says loudly. "I was just trying to be a good neighbor." He holds his arms out and looks around, as if to demonstrate to any passersby that he's been wronged.

I keep my voice quiet, steady, and firm. "Did you not

understand me? I asked you to go away and stop bothering me."

With a huff, he gives me one last glare before striding off. "Bitch!" he shouts as he leaves.

I let out my breath and wipe my sweaty hands on my pants. Regaining my composure, I begin backing up, only to realize that I've turned the wheel too far and the trailer is jackknifing. I'm told that these short trailers are trickier to maneuver than long ones, since they react so quickly to the slightest turn of the wheel. I pull forward to straighten it out and try again, turning very, very gently.

Moving at a snail's pace, I adjust left, then right, then left again ever so slightly until it looks like I've positioned my unit in exactly the spot it needs to be. "Yes!" I call out.

I hear applause and look up to see two women standing in the road, clapping.

"Great job," the taller one says.

"Not only on parking your camper, but on telling that jerk where to get off," the short one says. "He pulled something like that when Steph was setting up our screen tent and I was inside," she says, nodding toward her friend. "She didn't know how to get rid of him, but when I heard the stress in her voice, believe you me, I got rid of the creep. Nobody messes with my wife and gets away with it."

Maybe there's something about short women that makes them especially fierce when need be. She's no taller than Ruth, although she's built solid and looks like she could do some damage if need be.

Smiling, I introduce myself and learn that they are Steph and Kit from Los Angeles and they occupy site 97. "Come by for some chips and guac this afternoon, if you're around," Steph says.

"Thanks. I'll bring salsa and veggies and introduce you to my friend, Ruth, if that's okay." Oh, good – we'll get to tell our chipmunk *Guacamole Olympics* story to a new audience.

After rearranging everything again inside my camper, I lock up and walk down to Ruth's site. I'm finally getting used to finding her home when her truck isn't, but that brings up a concern. Will it be out of the shop before we're supposed to check out of Whispering Clouds on Monday? They told her the truck would be fixed within a week and tomorrow marks one week after her accident, but you know how that goes. Tomorrow will pass and then it'll be the weekend. If it's ready on Monday, we still have to drive into town to retrieve it, then return before 11 A.M. check out.

Ruth greets me with the answer to my unspoken questions. "Good news, dear. I just got a call from the body shop and they promise to have my truck ready for pick up tomorrow at 2:00."

What a relief! I'm not going to admit to Ruth that I'd gotten myself all worked up about this, since I know she'll just remind me not to fret so much about everything. *It'll all work out*, she'd say. *Worrying isn't going to change the outcome.* And I know she's right, but it's hard to reform my nature.

"What are your thoughts on glass blowing?" she asks.

"Uh ... I can't say that I actually have any thoughts on the subject," I say, wondering if she's considering taking up a new hobby or wants advice on a gift for someone.

"I'm thinking we could go watch artists create glass sculptures and then take a walk along the river. The couple in the teardrop camper told me about a park and trail we haven't visited yet, and the glass blowing shop. We can even try blowing molten glass ourselves!"

Oh, boy. Fiddling around with glass heated to a few thousand degrees – now that sounds like a recipe for disaster. I'm fine with watching the professionals do it, but I'll just be a spectator, thank you very much. Ruth, I know, will be the first to step forward if they ask for volunteers.

We agree to meet back at my vehicle in ten minutes. I'll

change shoes and bring along an apple and a small water bottle in my waist pack for our walk.

When I try to turn the key in the deadbolt lock on my camper's door, it won't budge. What's going on? That's the right key, isn't it? I check it and try again – still no luck. Switching to the other lock, I find that it turns easily. So it's definitely not a problem with the key. I think something's gone wrong with the deadbolt.

Okay, give it another shot. This time I put all my strength into it. No go. Fine – I just need more leverage. Fortunately, I carry a small toolkit in one of the storage areas accessible from outside the trailer, and even more fortunately, those doors use an entirely different key. Once I unload my tools and retrieve a pair of needle-nose pliers, I figure I'm good to go. I insert the door key again, get a death-grip on it with the pliers, and heave.

Snap!

Uh, oh. I'm left clenching half a key in my pliers – the other half is broken off inside the lock. Now what?

Ruth arrives as I'm staring despondently at the door.

"Is something wrong?"

After explaining the situation and showing her the non-business end of the broken key, I ponder what the cost of calling a locksmith out to the campground might be.

"I have another idea," Ruth says, peering into the access door I've left open. "Can you get to this storage area from inside the camper?"

"Yeah."

"I'm sure I can fit through here," she says, kneeling to get a better look inside. She starts hauling items out of the compartment and setting them on the pavement beside her.

"Hang on a minute, Ruth. Yes, I imagine you could crawl inside a ways, but then you'd have to turn ninety degrees around that divider you see and somehow push your way past all the stuff I've stored that you can't see from here, then kick open the interior door and slide out onto the floor in front of the kitchen. In other words, that's not going to work."

"Do you have a flashlight or headlamp?" she says, ignoring my conclusion.

With a sigh, I retrieve an extra headlamp I keep in my glove box.

Donning it, she sticks her upper body into the opening. I can hear her muffled voice declare, "I think this is going to work." She pulls back into the open air and stands up. "I may need you to give me a push at some point, so stay close by where you can hear me."

"Ruth! You don't have to do this. I'll just call a locksmith. And what about your neck? You shouldn't be straining it by crawling around like that."

She shakes her head, the motion much more normal than it was a few days ago. "My neck will be fine. Let's give this a shot."

Before I can think of another objection, she's placed my little stepstool beneath the compartment door and is most of the way inside the opening. "Push me in a little farther," she shouts, so I comply by grabbing her legs, which are sticking straight out of the trailer, and sliding her slowly forward until she hollers, "That's good. You can let go."

I wait anxiously as I hear occasional thumps and grunts coming from within. "Is everything okay?" I yell, and get a muted "Fine!" in return.

A woman walking a small dog approaches. "Is that your child crawling around in there?"

"No, just a very petite friend," I reply.

"Oh." Her eyes widen. "An adult? Oh my." I don't add that Ruth's in her 80s – she'd never believe me. "I can't image anybody fitting into that tiny hole. I'd get stuck for sure!"

"You and me, both," I say.

The dog starts whining, then barking at the sounds coming from the compartment, so the lady excuses herself and departs with the excited animal.

After a particularly loud thud, Ruth's voice calls out, "Ta da!" and moments later I hear noises just inside the door. "Can you unlock it?" I say, loudly. "It's the red thingy on the lock."

I hear rattling and more rattling. "It won't budge," she reports. "I'm going to unlatch the Dutch door so we can open it and talk more easily." The top half of the split door swings open and she's standing there grinning ear-to-ear, a film of dust streaking one side of her face and a strip of her otherwise royal blue shirt.

"Do you have a Phillips screwdriver and pliers?" she asks. "I think I might be able to turn the lock if I get inside the mechanism from here."

It's already broken, so how much more harm could she do? I may as well humor her before calling for professional help.

"Ta da again!" she declares after fussing with the tools for a minute. She opens the unlocked door and steps outside. "For now, why don't I put it back together and you can still use the regular lock. Just don't use the deadlock until you can get someone to fix it."

Wow. This lady never ceases to amaze me.

"Ready to go blow some molten glass?" she asks after finishing up.

"Sure. Why not?" She hasn't led me wrong so far.

Chapter 11

"Hey, Mom. It's me, your daughter."

As if anyone else would address me as *Mom*. "How are you and the kids? Anything new and exciting happen since we talked?"

"No, not really. Same old, same old. How about you? You been workin', or what?" she asks.

"Fortunately, I'm semi-retired now. I do some proofreading jobs here and there, but spend much of my time traveling and hiking. I actually live out of my little camper full time! Can you believe it?"

"Really? Like you don't have a house or apartment or nothin'?"

"Not any more. I've been living 'on the road' so to speak for a few years now, and I love it!" I say, looking around the interior of my A-Roamer and grinning. This is home. "What about you? Where do you all live?"

"Newark, New Jersey. We got a two bedroom apartment, so me and Emily used to share one room till Michael went off to college. Now there's more space. Emily wants to go to a local school, so she'll still be livin' here with me. Assumin' things work out."

I've thought some more about offering funds to help Emily with her college plans, but it feels a bit premature to bring that up now. We've barely scratched the surface in getting to know each other, and I don't want to make Lisa feel awkward or possibly insulted by my assumption that they could use some financial assistance.

"What is she planning on majoring in?" I ask.

She hesitates before answering. "Oh, she's not sure yet. Maybe some sort of science. She's done real good in her science classes in high school. I guess you musta been real good in English when you went to school, right, since you're a proofreader and all?"

I smile, remembering my favorite high school teacher, Mrs. Unger. I had her for English literature one year and English composition the next. She could be extremely tough on us, assigning massive chunks of reading materials and challenging us to dig deeply into tomes that are more often tackled in college. But she saw something in me, and helped me believe in my writing ability. After many years as a technical writer, I transitioned into proofreading both fiction and non-fiction. "I loved English. How about you? What was your favorite subject?"

"Oh, lots of subjects. I don't know. It don't matter much now, though. I answer phones in an office durin' the day and wait tables at night. History and math don't help me much day to day. Of course I'm thrilled that the kids are gonna be able to do much more with their education than I ever did." She pauses for a moment. "So, anyways I was wonderin' if you went to college. After havin' a baby and all when you was in high school, I guess you probably got kinda behind in your studies, right?"

"Well, your arrival date actually worked out fairly well in that respect. I finished out 10th grade, disappeared to an aunt's home in Iowa for the summer, and gave birth to you several weeks before my junior year began. I suppose I should thank you for that," I say, hoping the comment comes across as light-hearted as I intended.

"Well, glad I didn't inconvenience you too much."

I can't quite read her tone – it's so flat. Is she just responding with another quip or is she hurt? How stupid of me to joke about something like that. "Lisa, I didn't mean for that to come out like it did. I'm sorry. You weren't simply an 'inconvenience.' The truth is, I was terrified. I couldn't begin to imagine how I would take care of a baby. Back in those days, girls who were pregnant couldn't stay in school, but I managed to hide my pregnancy for long enough to finish up tenth grade. Or at least before my teachers could no longer pretend they hadn't noticed my baby bump. There were few paths for girls who kept their babies to ever get a high school diploma. Your father was even younger than I was, and his family pulled him out of that school and moved away. My parents convinced me that you would have a much better chance at a good future if you were adopted by two adults with the financial and emotional means of raising a child. And I believe they were right."

Silence. Then, finally, "Hey, I get it, Mom. Like, if Emily had got knocked up when she was fifteen, I know she couldn't have raised a kid on her own, and it woulda been pretty damn hard for me to feed another mouth. So, I get it. No worries."

I let out a long breath. "So, how were things for you, growing up?"

"It was good. Mama and Pop were almost forty when they adopted me, and they were good parents. We had a nice home and they really loved me. So, I think you did the right thing. It's just too bad you won't ever get to meet them," she says, her voice tight.

"I'm sorry about that as well. But," I say, trying to turn the conversation to something more upbeat, "now I'll get to meet you and the kids, which is very exciting! I'd love to make some plans to get out your way to visit in person. Or we could meet somewhere out west where I've been spending my time. Any ideas about when we could do that?"

"Oh. Yeah, that would be really great. But I'm not sure when we could all get together. You know, with Michael workin' and Emily about to start college if we ... well, probably that'll happen. Or she'll maybe have to start workin' someplace full time. But for sure, yeah. We'll figure something out."

I've got to be more realistic. They have their own lives. The kids might not even be all that interested in meeting their "new" grandma. "I understand completely. Maybe for now you and I should just work on finding a time and place where the two of us can meet. I would love to see you face-to-face!"

"Oh, for sure! Let me think about that. I don't have any vacation time with my office job for another four months, but ... well, I'll see what I can work out."

Figuring a change of subject is needed, I ask, "Did you get that loan application sent off okay?"

"Oh, yeah. Now it's just a waitin' game, right?" She sighs. "I sure hope her loan comes through. I've squeezed every little bit I can from my savings and we still come up short. I'm worried that they won't approve the whole amount we asked for. And then I worry about how she'll ever pay it back if they *do* approve the whole amount! You know how kids are strugglin' these days with these gignormous loans – like they'll never manage to pay them off. Or ever be able to buy a house, or nothin'. Even with good jobs. It's tragic, you know?"

"I agree." Biting my lip, I decide to plunge in. "Lisa, let me ask you something, and please give me an honest answer. Would it help you and Emily if I sent you a little money to help her get started in college? Not a loan, you understand. A gift."

"Oh my God. Mom! I ... are you sure you want to do that? That's so kind of you, but I can't ask you to send money."

I blink away the tears forming in my eyes. "Well, you didn't ask me, now did you? I offered. Please let me do this for you, Lisa. I would love to help Emily go to college."

I hear her sniff loudly. "Mom, thank you so much. This means so much to us. Uh – well, this is awkward – can I ask how much you're talkin' about?"

"I was thinking of five hundred dollars. Will that help? I don't know how much you're trying to borrow with the loan."

"Oh, Mom, that'll help a bunch. So, the loan we applied for is, um, ten thousand dollars. But five hundred will sure help. Really."

Oh, dear. That's not going to make much of a dent. And I can hear a trace of disappointment in her voice, although she's trying to hide it. Maybe I could manage a little bit more. I'll have to think about it.

"I'm glad. Let me get your address so I can mail you a check," I say, grabbing a pen and a small pad of paper.

"Sure – well, actually Mom, I kinda worry about how secure our mail is here. Like, it's pretty easy for someone to get into all our mailboxes and steal stuff. My next door neighbor – she had a tax refund check that didn't show up, but the IRS told her somebody cashed it. So how about you wire the money instead?"

"Oh, dear. Sure, I can do that. Do you know what information I'll need to give to my bank?"

"Yeah, no problem. I've had to do it before. You got somethin' to write with?"

She gives me her account information and asks if I do my bank business online or at a bank branch. With all the traveling I do, I use my bank's smartphone app, which seems to please her. "Sounds like you're pretty tech savvy," she says.

"Not all that much, but I do okay with a few odds and ends," I say. "I'll send the transfer as soon as we get off the phone," I tell her.

"Mom, I can't tell you how much this means to me and Emily. Thank you again."

We finish up with a promise from her that Emily will call

me to thank me personally. As soon as the call ends, I pull up my bank app and enter the transaction. My finger hovers over the *Send* button and I hesitate. Oh, what the heck. I change the dollar amount to $1,000 and complete the transaction. Not that a thousand dollars is a trivial amount to me, but I can manage it. This is for my granddaughter's future, after all. Over the past two years, I've been taking on fewer and fewer proofreading clients, but I could step that up a bit and still have plenty of time to enjoy myself. I can earn an extra grand with just a few additional manuscripts.

Meanwhile, I need to get busy preparing to finally move on to our camp near Crater Lake. Ruth's got her truck again and claims her neck is fine, so we're both excited to begin our next adventures. She's got a list of hikes and scenic drives that will surely keep us well occupied for our three week stay in the area. I can hardly wait!

Chapter 12

The color is incredible. Although I've seen pictures of Crater Lake many times, they can't do justice to the azure splendor of the expanse of water far below us. When we first drove up to the main parking area, we scurried up to the rim of the crater like children racing to be the first in line at the ice cream truck. Our initial glimpse of the lake exceeded all of our expectations.

"Breathtaking!" Ruth exclaims.

Literally. Even she sounds out of breath after our dash in the thin air. I'm huffing and puffing like the Big Bad Wolf. But just look at that water! I take about a dozen photos with my phone before Ruth is urging me to continue along the rim trail.

"Look, there's Wizard Island," she says, pointing at what looks like a miniature mountain floating in the vast lake. "That's where we'll be going next week."

"I see the boat!" I say, pointing at a vessel far below us, cutting through the still water and leaving a white wake trailing behind it. Wondering where the launch might be, I scan the perimeter of the water, searching for a road or path down from the crater rim. "How in the world do we get down to the boat?"

"There's a trail down to the water. Somewhere," Ruth says, sounding a bit puzzled as she, too, surveys the steep, rugged cliffs rising above the waters. "I imagine it'll be obvious when we get to the parking area for the boat tours."

We spend the rest of the day hiking out and back along different portions of the rim, driving to another vantage point, and walking another stretch. I can't get enough of the views and the shades of blue which shift with our vantage points and with the angle of the sun. Sapphire, royal blue, cobalt, cornflower, lapis, indigo – there aren't enough names to truly capture the spectacle.

Eventually too tired to walk any further, we decide to return to camp, saving further exploration of the trails and rim road for later this week.

Our campground is surrounded by thick forest – we almost missed finding its entrance off the two-lane highway. The road itself feels like something cut off from the rest of the world. Tall, dense evergreens line both sides, towering above so the effect is like driving through a long, dark tunnel. Except around high noon, the roadway remains deeply shadowed. The camp, however, is open enough for dappled sunlight on my picnic table in the afternoon and full sun shining through my windows in the cool of morning. In other words, a perfect setting. Ruth's site is almost across from mine, with a medium-sized motor home only partially blocking my view of her camper.

One thing I miss since becoming a full-time camper is cooking elaborate dishes. That's something I enjoyed when I lived in a home with a well-equipped kitchen including a large oven and a five-burner stove, a combo microwave and convection oven, an assortment of kitchen knives, a food processor, a rice steamer, bowls of all sizes, frying pans, a roasting pan, multiple saucepans, and on and on. In my little A-frame, to say that space is limited is an understatement. Besides, after fleeing my east coast home in the path of a hurricane and then being robbed, I had to start over with absolutely nothing.

Tonight, however, I've decided to prepare something special for dinner despite having a limited selection of kitchen tools at my disposal. An assortment of veggies are roasting on Ruth's small propane grill as I slice a rib eye steak into strips, season it, then add the meat to the grill. It'll be a simple meal, but a cut above our typical fare of spaghetti or mac and cheese or grilled chicken breast with a salad.

"Wow. Somebody's cooking something delicious," a man calls out as he and his wife stroll past my site.

I smile and wave, expecting them to continue past, but they step closer instead.

"And it *looks* as delicious as it smells," the woman says. "That seems like a lot of food for just one person. I'll bet you'll have some leftovers tonight."

It's an odd remark, but I go with the flow. "Actually, there are two of us, but you may be right. We probably won't manage to eat it all in one sitting."

"Well, enjoy yourselves then." They walk back to the road and continue their walk just as Ruth arrives, bringing a bottle of wine and two glasses, another special treat we don't indulge in very often.

"Those folks sure seemed impressed with your cooking, dear," she says, setting down the items and pulling a corkscrew from her pocket. "I think they were trying to finagle an invitation to dinner!"

The meal turned out great, but I did make too much food. Just as I step into my camper to fetch a container to store the leftovers, I hear voices outside. I peek out and sure enough, here's the hungry couple again.

"Looks like we were right," the man says. "That was way more than you could eat. You know, that looks and smells so great, would you mind if we help you finish that off?"

I stick my head out the door and Ruth and I look at each other, trying to read each other's expression. She shrugs slightly, her eyes widening as if to ask, *What do you think we should do?*

Hey, maybe they're down on their luck and have been subsisting on nothing but ramen noodles. What the heck — let them have the rest of the meal.

"Sure," I say, "we're glad to share. Let me get out some paper bowls to send that home with you."

"Oh, that's okay," the woman says. "We'll just eat it here."

They proceed to sit down at the table, pick up our used silverware before I can offer clean ones, and chow down. Ruth and I glance at each other in shock, then struggle to avoid bursting into laughter.

After wolfing down all the remaining food, they rise from the table. "Thanks. That was delicious!" she says.

"I'm glad you enjoyed it," I say. "I'm Ellie, by the way, and this is my friend, Ruth."

"Thanks again, Ellie and Ruth. Have a great evening," the man says, and they're off.

Once they're out of earshot, Ruth says, "Nice meeting you, too, Mr. and Mrs. No Name. Stop by again when you can stay a while."

We giggle, then clean up the dishes and grill before starting on our evening stroll. Almost immediately, we encounter the No Names again, camped just a few sites over from me. They're sitting outside a monster motorhome that I recognize as a very high-end model, one that can cost half a million dollars or more. Ruth and I wave and they stare at us blankly, as if having no idea who we are. Huh. I'm thinking they can afford more than ramen. Although, maybe after paying for that luxury RV, there's no money left for food.

As we circle the campground, we check out everyone's units, chatting with those folks sitting outside enjoying the mild evening, and dodging the small parade of children running a mini-Indy 500 on bikes, tricycles, and roller skates around the campground driving loops. They circle past us several times, the volume of their exuberance increasing with each lap as additional little ones joining the race.

"I hope they quiet down before my bedtime," I say after a little girl screams at the top of her lungs as she hurls past.

"I'm sure it'll be fine," Ruth says. "They'll wear themselves out. Too bad there isn't a playground or anything here for them. No real place for them to gather to play catch or tag."

Many of the large, commercial campgrounds do have places set aside for children to play safely. We've already seen a pickup hauling a trailer arrive, pulling around a curve only to be suddenly surrounded by a swarm of small kids. Fortunately, he saw them in time to stop.

"I think I'll call it a day – go tuck myself in and read for a bit before bed," Ruth says as we approach our sites again. "Have a good night."

That sounds like a fine idea. My legs are tired, the light is rapidly fading, and as Ruth predicted, the shouts of the little ones have faded away. I manage to read for a half hour or so, then prepare for bed. Another day of adventure awaits.

Chapter 13

As I tie back the curtains and peer outside to see what the early morning will bring, I gasp in wonder at the sight of three deer grazing just outside my camper. Moving very slowly and quietly, I lean close to the window and realize there are more – many more. Eight – no, eleven. I click off a few photos through the glass, then open the curtains on the opposite side and am rewarded with the discovery of even more of the graceful animals, munching calmly on the grasses and leaves of the bushes surrounding my campsite. Although I know it's hard to see into my camper's tinted windows, I remain as still as I can. A doe raises her head up high and her long, mule-like ears rotate in my direction. I hold my breath. She steps away in slow motion, impossibly thin legs stilting her toward a much smaller animal – perhaps her own fawn.

Then, in a snap, something grabs the attention of the herd. They all turn their heads in the same direction and – boom – they're off and running, bouncing like they're on pogo sticks and disappearing into the forest.

Wow. What an amazing way to start my day. I can hardly wait to tell Ruth!

Pulling on a light jacket, I venture outside where I'll be

able to see the front door of her camper. Wouldn't you know it – she's already up and outside, perched on her rainbow-striped yoga mat which is colorful even in this dim, early morning light. I stroll over and she greets me with, "Ellie – you just missed seeing a beautiful herd of deer! There must have been at least thirty of them bounding right past me. I didn't move a muscle and they never even glanced my way."

We rave about our experience all through a shared breakfast of scrambled eggs and toast. Charli, it seems, didn't share our enthusiasm for all those tall animals. She hid under Ruth's camper as they passed. However, the cat is more than happy to partake in a dab of eggs and to lick the butter off a corner of toast that I may or may not have dropped on purpose.

***

Returning from our rather strenuous hike to the top of a peak overlooking Crater Lake, my phone beeps, signaling me that I have a missed call. There must be service at the beautiful lodge we're walking past on the way back to our car. I pause to check who called, and my weariness disappears when I see Lisa's number displayed.

"Let's stop here for a minute so I can try to call my daughter back," I say to Ruth. She's quite willing to find a spot to sit and continue admiring the views.

"Lisa," I say when she answers. "Sorry I missed your call earlier. There's very little cell service around here, but I've found a spot that works."

"Hey, Mom. If you've got a minute, Emily wants to talk to you."

I perk up even more. "That's great! Put her on!"

My heart is thumping with excitement – my pulse rate may be as high now as it was when we climbed up that rocky section of the trail! Pressing my phone against my ear and my free hand against the other, I try to hear over the sound of two men talking loudly on the lodge's nearby patio.

"Hello? Grandma?"

Oh my God. It's my granddaughter! "Yes, hello Emily. I'm so happy to hear your voice."

"You too, Grandma. Mama's been telling us all about you."

I blink rapidly. "You know, you sound almost exactly like your mother on the phone."

She giggles in a nervous sort of way. "Yeah, people tell us that a lot. Like, when my girlfriends come over and Mama and me are in the kitchen and Mama hollers, 'Anybody want a soda?' they'll think it's me instead."

"I can understand that. So, Emily, are you excited about starting college soon?"

"Definitely. So, like that's the big reason I wanted to talk to you. To thank you for sending money for school. That's like huge! Thank you, Grandma."

"I'm glad to do it. I wish you all the best with your future plans. Speaking of which, any further news about your loan application?"

"Nuh uh, but maybe we'll hear something before the weekend. And listen, Grandma. If things don't work out so I can afford college this semester, I'm gonna pay you back."

"Oh, Emily, that isn't at all necessary. I'd love for the money to go toward school, but if that doesn't work out, it's still yours to keep." What a fine young woman she is to even bring that up! Now I feel even better about giving her the money.

"Okay, Grandma. Thank you. You're the best!" she declares. Then, "Um, listen – Mama wants her phone back so hang on. Thanks again. See ya."

I hope "see ya" actually means she'd like to meet in person. "You're welcome, Emily." Hearing nothing on her end, I'm not sure if she's still on the line. Maybe she's handed the phone to Lisa. "Hello?" I say as the silence continues. "Are you there?" I wonder if the call has dropped. Before I pull the phone away from my face to check the indicator, I hear a voice.

"Hey, Mom. I'm back. Listen, I was just on my way out the door, so I gotta cut this short, but we'll talk again soon, okay?"

Maybe it's just as well. This is hardly the ideal setting for having a conversation that feels intensely personal to me in a location where I'm having difficulty hearing over the voices around me. I'm not the only person to have discovered this hot spot for catching up on calls and messages.

Seeing me stow my phone back in my pocket, Ruth approaches. "That was short. I figured you'd talk longer."

"Short but sweet," I answer as we stroll toward the parking lot. "I'll have you know that I was addressed as 'Grandma' for the very first time!"

"No kidding? Well, just one glance at your face and I can tell that was a really special thrill for you. It's pretty darn special to be a grandma."

"I'm starting to feel that. Of course, it's not like getting to babysit and watch them grow up, like you've done with your four grandsons."

She reaches out and hugs me. "It's special no matter how you look at it. All my boys are adults now, but I still feel all warm and fuzzy when one of them calls me Grandma. Enjoy it. Just a word of warning – you'll want to spoil your grandkids rotten, but try to control yourself." She laughs, tossing her pack into the back of her truck. "That's one of the hardest parts about being a grandparent!"

I smile, wondering what she'd say if she knew how much I'm already "spoiling" my granddaughter. I'm not sure why I haven't told her about my gift yet. Maybe she'll think I went overboard. And maybe she's right. But I'll bet she's spent more than a thousand dollars over the years on each of her grandkids. I'm just playing catch up. And goodness knows the money is for a very good cause, not just for a new toy or sweater.

I'm sure I'll end up telling Ruth about the money at some point. Maybe after Emily hears back on that loan and knows if she'll be starting college next month.

***

Incredibly, Mr. and Mrs. No Name With the Expensive RV just happen to wander over to my site again as we're finishing supper. Ironically, we prepared ramen tonight, although we jazzed it up with grilled chicken and added diced carrots and green bell peppers.

The man comments on how wonderful our meal smells, and this time she whips out a pair of metal mess kits from a tote she's carrying. They look like something from an army surplus store. "We remembered to bring our own bowls and forks this time," the woman says, smiling.

When neither Ruth nor I make a move to offer the remaining pot of noodles to them, they look puzzled. "Sorry," I say, "it looks like we're going to finish all our meal tonight."

"Oh," she says, stretching her neck to try to see how much is left in the pot.

Ruth pretends not to notice and slaps the lid closed. "Keeping it warm," she says, smiling at the people. "Now, you folks have a lovely evening."

I follow up with, "So long. It was nice of you to stop by."

Thankfully, they get the message and wander off, possibly in search of another group to feed them.

"Maybe neither one knows how to cook?" Ruth says.

"Or how to heat up a frozen dinner in the microwave."

"Maybe their refrigerator is on the fritz."

"Sure, it could be something like that," I say. "Or maybe they're just weird."

"Being weird has never slowed me down," she says, grinning. "Think how boring life would be if we never met any weird people!"

Good point.

Chapter 14

Franklin would have loved this. Ruth and I have just descended a steep, switchbacked trail from the rim down to the lake, where we'll be boarding a tour boat shortly that will take us out to Wizard Island. We'll have several hours to explore the island and we've rented fishing gear to try our luck at catching some of the fish that were stocked in the waters over a hundred years ago. Franklin always enjoyed fishing, although I never understood the draw. Still, I'm willing to give it a try.

Ruth and I plan to hike the trail on the island to its top, which is also carved out with a volcanic crater – a miniature volcano within a volcano. All in all, this will be a fairly strenuous day, but I'm reassured by the fact that we'll have a considerable amount of time to rest on the boat again after our island hike before we tackle climbing back up to the main rim and our vehicle.

It's fascinating how different the lake looks from way down here. I hadn't really grasped the drop in elevation from the rim to the water – everything is much larger than I had expected. We climb aboard the tour boat and snatch two seats that we hope will offer the best views. Once fully loaded up, we launch, marveling at the crystal clear view of the shallow rocks beneath us. Shortly, though, we're in deeper waters.

As we enjoy the cool breeze off the water on this very warm morning, a park ranger tells us about the lake. What lies below us is still a bit of a mystery, as the water depth reaches nearly 2,000 feet. The thought makes me shudder in awe. Mount Mazama, a volcano which erupted almost eight thousand years ago, formed this caldera which eventually filled with water.

The island looms high above us as we approach and I wonder how we'll possibly make our way to its top. Some of its slopes are tree-covered, while much of it appears to be covered with loose volcanic rocks. Once we land, the start of the trail is obvious and we decide to tackle the hike right away. We find a place to stow our fishing gear and head upward.

A few fit-looking folks from the boat start up the trail as well. One couple, possibly in their late thirties, take off running and are out of sight in no time, their long, muscular legs carrying them along like they are flying. "Wonder Woman and Superman are probably at the top already," Ruth says, moving along at a pretty impressive pace.

"Good," I pant. "Maybe they can revive me when I collapse up there. Can we slow down just a bit?"

When Ruth and I first met, I was the epitome of a couch potato – out of shape, overweight, and certain that I couldn't do a thing about it, with my advanced age of 60 fast approaching. Observing an octogenarian who does yoga every morning and hikes three or four times a week forced me to reconsider. She encouraged and coached me, so now, at 62, I'm in pretty decent shape, about 20 pounds lighter than I was, and I still can't quite keep up with the woman!

We continue up the switchbacks at a more manageable pace, stepping carefully on the volcanic trail surface. When we reach the top, we gaze down into the island's own caldera, this one dry, unlike Mount Mazama's caldera containing the spectacular lake.

"Pretty cool, isn't it?" Wonder Woman offers us an enormous smile, then assumes a one-legged position with her arched back and free leg creating almost a perfect circle, her foot grasped with both hands above her head. Superman snaps a few shots of her, framed in front of the gorgeous watery backdrop.

"How can she bend like that?" I whisper to Ruth.

"She's quite good," she whispers back. "I used to be able to get into Dancer's Pose about twenty years ago, but my shoulders just aren't as flexible as they used to be."

In other words, when she was my age, she was like Wonder Woman, here. Only much, much shorter.

After descending, we find a good spot to enjoy the scenery and, almost as an afterthought, plunk our lines into the water. We don't catch anything, which is just fine with me. I had no intention of carrying dead fish back on the boat and up the long trail out of here, nor did I want to attempt to remove my hook from a slimy, wriggling fish. I'm just saying.

By mid-afternoon we arrive back at the main dock, slightly sunburned and windblown. Ruth manages to get into conversations with many of the people we encounter who are heading down the trail to play around in the cold water or simply to enjoy a different perspective. I'm thankful for her congeniality – we are taking frequent breaks instead of rushing back up the steep path, so I can easily keep up with her.

"What an incredible day!" she says as we climb into my Jeep. "I'm so glad we did this."

On the way back to camp, we treat ourselves to ice cream cones. "When my girls were little," Ruth says, "I would have told them it was too close to dinnertime for ice cream. But now that we're seniors," she says with a wink, "the hell with rules like that! Like they say, 'Life's short. Eat dessert first.'"

"Hear, hear," I say and we pretend to clink our cones

together like wine glasses.

Once back at camp, the children's drag races are in full swing again. The youngest participants from last night don't seem to be around, but there are several older kids who've joined the chaos. At one point, seconds before I was about to swing my camper door open to step outside, a boy on a scooter zips through my campsite at arm's length from the wall of my trailer. If I had opened the door a moment earlier, it would have taken him out.

I consider going to the office and complaining about the children being out of control, but my imagination suddenly conjures a fantasy of a younger version of myself watching over my two small grandchildren at play. Would I have been the sort of grandma who was always hovering over the kids, fussing at them whenever they were too boisterous? I'm not around children very often and I know I'm not as patient or forgiving of their exuberance as I could be. True, it's rude and possibly dangerous to ride through someone else's site, but maybe I can learn to be a bit less uptight about it all.

Meanwhile, I rearrange my camp chair and the angle of the picnic table so any future shortcut through my site won't be such a close shave.

After a late, light dinner, I don my headlamp for my final visit to the ladies' restroom before turning in. Some women I've met out camping are astonished that I can survive without a bathroom inside my unit, but I don't find it to be much of an issue. Even overnight, I have a handy-dandy, collapsible toilet which works fine for those times my bladder refuses to wait until morning. I just pour some magic powder inside the plastic bag liner and there's no nastiness to deal with. Ruth suggested I try using kitty litter in my system instead, but I assured her this works far better for humans.

Either my light has grown dimmer or my night vision is getting worse. With no moon in view, the campground is incredibly dark, save for a few campsites where folks have laid out a glowing, blue circle of lights beneath their campers. Which is fine for finding *their* campsites, but doesn't help me navigate the loop to the bathroom.

Much to my dismay, my headlamp fails entirely just as I emerge from the restroom. There's enough light cast by the fixture just outside the door, but once I reach the gravel campground road, I can barely make out my hand in front of my face. Looking around, I spot a few scattered glimpses of light through the trees and bushes, but not enough to guide me.

Maybe if I wait by the bathroom, someone will come by with a light and they'll walk me back to my site. It seems like the best plan, but after ten minutes of pacing outside the door – at least my *watch* illuminates – I grow impatient. The problem is that almost all the other RVs in this campground probably have their own toilets, so it's quite possible that nobody else will be visiting the restroom tonight. So, I guess I'm going to have to just try to find my way back in the dark.

Stepping carefully, I listen and feel for a change in the road surface under my sneakers while trying to visualize exactly how soon the path curves. Thinking I'm close to the left edge of the paved road, I almost stumble as my right foot slips off into the dirt and I get a face full of leaves. I sidle further toward what I hope is the center of the road, then scoot a foot forward again, my arms reaching out in front of me to warn if I'm about to walk into another shrub.

I can imagine the headline now – Woman Spends Night Wandering in Circles in the Dark. The article would include a photo of me, branches and twigs dangling from my tangled hair, with a useless headlamp perched on my forehead like a third eye.

Eventually, guided by the glow of somebody's campfire far ahead, I spot a neighbor's display of low, solar lanterns leading to their door. I thought I was much closer to my own place, but now at least I'm reoriented and know I've meandered too far right again. It only takes me a few more minutes before I locate the distinctive yellow porch light of my own unit. Lucky thing that I remembered to turn it on as I left – I often forget.

As I crawl into bed, I feel like I've just completed some Olympian feat. Tomorrow's first task: put new batteries in my headlamp.

Chapter 15

"Still no word on the loan?" I'm quite surprised, since I would expect the fall term to start very soon. How can a student enroll in classes with their funding still up in the air?

"Nothin'," Lisa says, "but I'm callin' them first thing tomorrow morning. Emily is a wreck, waitin' to hear. And the school wants full payment by the end of the week, or she'll have to withdraw." She sighs in dismay. "That'll break her heart."

I ask if there's anything I can do, but of course there isn't. "You've already done so much to help, Mom. I'll find out what's goin' on. Catch them first thing at the start of a new work week."

She promises to let me know what happens, then our conversation turns to learning more of each other's history. We realize that we both enjoy hiking and gardening. "I help with a flower garden at our church," she tells me. I talk about when I used to volunteer at the Botanical Gardens near my home when I lived in California. She dreams of visiting some of the National Parks, so I tell her about the boat tour here at Crater Lake and relay stories from some of the other parks I've been to.

"Call or send me a message when you know more about Emily's loan," I remind her just before we finish up.

***

Tonight is ice cream social night at the campground. When Ruth and I arrive, we see that the camp hosts have set out three large tubs of ice cream – chocolate, strawberry, and vanilla. They do the serving as campers pass through a long line, adding fudge or caramel syrup, chopped nuts, maraschino cherries, and whipped topping as desired. We both opt for chocolate ice cream, but I refrain from adding more than a smidgeon of fudge to mine. Ruth goes whole hog on her dessert. The woman claims she's never been able to gain weight, no matter how she tries. I've offered to give her ten of my own pounds anytime she wants them. Heck, let's go for twenty and I'll be down to my college freshman weight again!

We sit on a bench set in a circle of seats and visit with our fellow campers. Bev and Albert are from Vancouver, British Columbia and are just out for a three week jaunt through Washington and Oregon. Bev is pregnant and I consider her huge belly nervously. Is it wise to be out camping when she might give birth soon?

Ruth may have the same concern as she asks when the baby is due.

"Oh, not for another eight weeks," Bev says, smiling. "I know – I'm enormous already. But look at her daddy!" She nods at Albert on the bench beside her. If he didn't play basketball or football in school, I'd be surprised. When they arrived, it was impossible not to notice the man towering over everyone else, especially his pretty wife who is about my modest height, five foot five. That's going to be one big baby.

"Will she be your first?" Ruth asks.

"Yes," they answer in chorus, beaming.

Bev frowns and sighs, "Sorry – got to go visit the little

girls' room. Again." Her husband helps her to her feet and she waddles away.

Albert sighs deeply. "I'll sure be glad when the baby finally comes and our lives can get back to normal."

The circle of people erupts in laughter. "Dude," a man with a frizzy, gray beard says, "trust me on this. Your lives will never 'get back to normal' again, even once your little girl is grown up."

Albert smiles sheepishly, then excuses himself to get another helping of ice cream. More people arrive and we start up introductions again. Helen and Penelope both teach elementary school and hail from Houston. We're just about to hear where Vince is from when the group bursts out laughing and I feel a gentle pressure on my shoulder.

"Charli, no. You can't have Ellie's ice cream." Ruth sets hers beside her on the bench – the side farthest from her cat, who has her rear end still perched on my shoulder as she walks her front feet down my chest and tries for another taste of my dessert. She looks up at Ruth, a blob of chocolate hiding most of her little, pink nose, and meows in protest as she is lifted away from the treat.

"Can I give her the last of mine?" Penelope asks, offering the melted remains of her ice cream by setting the paper bowl on the ground.

"As long as it isn't chocolate," Ruth says, releasing her pet. Charli scurries over to the vanilla offering, determined to lap it up before "mom" changes her mind.

"I can't take you anywhere," Ruth quips, shaking her head as she grins down at Charli, who has already licked the bowl so clean you can't tell it has ever been used. She peers up at the sea of human admirers, vocalizing her request for more bowls to scrub spotless. Ruth retrieves her and gives her a quick snuggle before placing her firmly on her lap and lovingly blocking the cat's attempt to escape. After a minute of disagreement between person and animal, Ruth decides the only way to prevent Charli from nagging everyone for sweets that might harm her is to retreat back to her camper. The party seems to be breaking up anyway, so we offer our goodbyes and return to our respective homes.

***

The campground population has thinned considerably now that the weekend has passed, and the throngs of children seem to have moved on to other destinations. Ruth and I continue exploring the National Park but also expand to discovering the wonders of the surrounding region. We hike within the lush forests to view lovely cascading waterfalls, delighting in the rich, loamy smells of our verdant surroundings. We discover water-carved boulders in a river and a dramatic view of a gorge carved by the thundering water. The roar echoing off the rocky walls is so loud that we spook a woman who was already standing on the bridge, peering down at the whitewater below. She didn't hear us approaching and shrieked, jumping backward and grasping her chest, when she glanced up and realized we were standing beside her. We apologize, feeling terrible for giving her such a fright, but she insists that she is fine. Good thing the railing is high enough that she didn't accidentally tumble off the bridge when we spooked her.

After so much time spent camping in desert environments during colder weather, we are captivated by all the water features and greenery of this region. "Let's go on a raft trip!" Ruth says, scrolling through information on her phone as we talk about our plans for tomorrow.

I hesitate. I've seen videos of people being thrown out of rafts as they plummet through raging waters. It looks terrifying. "I was hoping for something a little more low key," I say. "Like another boat tour on a calm lake."

Her eyes glint with excitement. "You've got to take a look

92

at this, Ellie. Very calm and low key. Listen," she says, reading from the screen, "'Suitable for the entire family. Relax as we float over gentle riffles and long stretches of calm waters. Your guide does all the paddling, so just sit back and enjoy the scenery. Don't forget your camera!' Doesn't that sound marvelous?"

Gentle riffles. Actually, that does sound marvelous. Ruth has managed to drag me along on several adventures that I never would have chosen for myself, but this seems right up my alley. "Let's give it a shot."

She calls the outfitter and books our spots for tomorrow afternoon for a half day of river rafting. We decide to have an early lunch picnic by a lake along the way, and I return to my camper to make preparations for tomorrow's adventure.

***

After checking in for our raft trip, our guide — a thin young man named Lucas, with long hair tied atop his head in a man-bun — has our group of four introduce ourselves. We'll be riding the raft with Melissa and her young daughter, Lily, who announces that she is eight years old. "How old are *you*?" she asks, looking quizzically at Ruth.

"Lily! You're being rude!" Melissa admonishes her.

"Oh, that's okay. I don't mind one little bit," Ruth says. "I'm eighty-two. How about that? I'll bet that's way older than even your grandma, right?"

The child shrugs. "I dunno. I guess so."

When you're eight, anything older than twenty probably seems ancient. "Remember back in the sixties and seventies when we used to say, 'Don't trust anyone over thirty'?" I say.

The two young adults and the little girl look at me with blank expressions on their faces. Of course they don't remember that saying. None of them was even born by the seventies. Probably not the eighties, either. I can almost hear

Melissa thinking, "Okay, boomer," but of course she doesn't say it out loud.

We listen to a talk on safety and then Lucas helps us strap on bulky orange life jackets. "Everybody ready for an awesome time?" he asks. We give an enthusiastic cheer and line up to climb onto the raft, which he has just pushed off from the shore. He stands in the water and offers Ruth a hand as she steps aboard.

"I gotta go to the bathroom," Lily announces. Her mother rolls her eyes and kneels down to discuss this with her child.

"You just told me you didn't have to go," Melissa says in a weary tone.

"I didn't then. Now I do."

"We're good," Lucas says, helping Ruth back to shore and yanking the raft partway out of the water. "No problem. We can wait."

Since Lily is wearing a one-piece swimsuit, she must be extracted from her life jacket before departing with her mom to the restroom.

"Carol used to do that every time we were heading out on a trip, whether it was just across town or a long drive for vacation," Ruth says. "In the mornings, especially, that child could go pee a half dozen times and still insist she needed to go once more right after we got in the car. Then, wouldn't you know it, she'd insist that David stop the car at the very next gas station or rest area we'd see."

Ah, kids. Naturally, all my adult life I've listened to stories of funny or cute or clever things my friends' children had done, but now I'm imagining myself in those parent roles, with Lisa or with my grandchildren. How would I have handled things? Would I have scolded the kid for holding up our group? Or just accepted it with a sigh, like Melissa did? I don't know the answer.

Once they return and Lily is strapped back into her orange

vest, we begin the boarding process again. Things go smoothly this time, although I partially lose my balance as I prepare to sit in the raft and plop down hard on the inflated seat, causing the raft to wobble precariously, or so it feels to me.

"Whee!" Lily shouts in response. Great. The highlight of her rafting adventure might be when one of the old ladies nearly capsizes the boat.

"Let's do this!" Lucas shouts, gracefully vaulting into the raft and taking his place with the oars. We begin to float and he guides us out to the middle of the river.

We glide between rocky shores with dense forests leading up the slopes, the rich, blue sky far above. A stone outcropping stretches from the bank as if reaching for the other shore, but Lucas steers us around it, the water forced to detour and rippling in response to the obstacle. Although I expected a rough ride through that section, the slight bounce of our raft is actually quite mild and I relax my death grip on a handle by my seat.

"Isn't this lovely!" Ruth says, her smile lighting up her face. She leans over the edge of the raft, scoops up a handful of water, and spills it on her head. Droplets glisten off her short, white hair above her bright blue visor. Feeling the heat of the sun, the rest of us follow suit, Melissa sprinkling river water on her daughter since her arms are too short to reach the water safely. She squeals in delight.

The outfitters have loaned us waterproof sleeves for our phones, so I take full advantage and snap dozens of photos of the scenery, my raft-mates, and our guide wielding the oars. When we pull into shore, it feels like our adventure has barely begun, but then I check the time and realize we've been floating for almost three hours.

As we ride the shuttle van back upstream to our starting point, Ruth keeps up a steady conversation with little Lily, discussing such diverse topics as whales, Lily's soccer team, favorite TV shows, princesses, and designing a recipe for the world's best chocolate chip cookies (secret ingredient: marshmallows). I'm generally awkward with children, grasping for topics that might engage them after the standards *How old are you?* and *What grade are you in?* I ask her what her favorite part of today's raft trip was, and her response is, "When you pretended to fall down and it made the whole boat jump around." See – I knew it! Perhaps I can start a new career in slapstick comedy.

Heading back to our campground, I let Ruth know that tomorrow will need to be a work day for me. I've just received a new manuscript to proofread, and I want to try to finish the job quickly so I can replenish my savings account. This one appears to be a lot more enjoyable than the last, so I'm actually looking forward to tackling it.

Chapter 16

Four tents, a jumble of children's bicycles and toys, and a picnic table loaded down with large plastic bins, a camp stove, lanterns, and two cases of beer fill the campsite next to mine. Three cars are squeezed into a space that was designed for two. But there's not a soul around.

I've just returned from running errands in the nearest town – stocking up on groceries, filling the Jeep with gas, and calling my latest client to discuss an additional job he may send my way. Phone service in camp is spotty, and I didn't want the call dropping in the middle of our conversation.

It's Saturday evening and the quiet we've enjoyed during the week has retreated. Eyeing the clues in the next site, I fear we'll be subjected to not only the commotion of small children playing, but an exuberant adult get-together as well. In my experience, combining a large group with booze doesn't usually equate to a quiet gathering.

As Ruth and I take our evening stroll around the grounds, we discover another site filled with revelers. They've aligned multiple tables with the picnic table, and it appears that they are preparing a feast for the dozen or so adults mingling about.

Children from toddlers to early teens are dashing about, dodging among the parents in a game of tag, or some such. Three of them snatch up bikes and ride past us, nearly rolling over our toes. Reggae music fills the air.

"Lucky thing we're at the other end of the loop," Ruth says. "I didn't hear any of this until we came around the curve."

Somehow, I have a suspicion that the "missing" group from the site next to mine might all be part of this huge gathering. If I'm lucky, they'll party over here and be ready for bed when they return to their tents. But if I'm unlucky ... well, I'll try to take Ruth's advice and not fret about that.

After our walk, we each retreat to our campers for a quiet evening. I compose a message for Lisa, telling her about our raft trip earlier this week and the scenic drive yesterday. I ask again for any news of Emily's college loan. After pressing 'send', I'm disappointed to see that the connection is bad again tonight, and the text message isn't being sent. I'll check again in the morning.

Later, I'm awakened by the sound of loud conversation. Damn. It's the people next door, back from their party, I suppose. When I hear children's voices as well, I check the time. Really, people? You've kept the kiddos up until midnight? The kids sound like they've just been wound up tight and released. I imagine they might have fallen asleep at the big party, then were awakened to walk back to camp, and now they're wired. After about fifteen minutes of parents scolding and children whining, things seem to settle down and I don't hear the kids any more. Good – they've put them to bed.

Although I can still hear talking, I stuff in my earplugs and the noise fades to a faint murmur. I doze off.

A woman's screeching laugh brings me awake again. They all must be much louder than before – I can hear several voices clearly through my plugged ears. I sit up and move a curtain aside just a smidge to see what's going on. An enormous fire lights up several faces while other people are in silhouette. Three people are standing close to my camper, talking loudly and with great animation, beer bottles in hand. One is the woman with the horribly loud laugh. They all turn toward the fire and hurl their beer bottles into the flames, screaming and hooting. A man delivers new beverages to the group and they clank them together hard enough that I'm surprised the bottles don't break.

I sigh and look at my watch. It's now almost 1:30 in the morning and it doesn't look like they'll be shutting things down anytime soon. What about those kids trying to sleep? Don't they even care about their own children?

There's a posted quiet time of 10:00 P.M. until 7:00 A.M., but I don't know who to contact about the ruckus. I'm sure the camp office is closed, and I'm uncertain where the staff stay, although there are two buildings near the office that seem to be residences. I turn on a light, glad that my black-out curtains won't reveal my actions, and I locate the information sheet I was given when I checked into camp, searching for a phone number to call after hours. Got it. Picking up my phone, I start to place a call, but it drops immediately. No service.

I could get dressed, grab my headlamp, and walk down to the office to see if I can figure out how to find the person on duty. Unfortunately, that would mean walking right past the partiers coming and going. So if I succeed in finding someone to get them to settle down, they're going to know who reported them. As a lone woman in the camper next door, I don't feel very comfortable with a gathering of drunk people possibly plotting revenge on the snitch. Even hightailing it over to Ruth's place in the hopes that their commotion isn't as bad over there doesn't seem like a good move. I'd still have to pass the revelers, and I'd likely scare the dickens out of my friend by showing up at her doorstep at this hour.

Wrapping a shirt around my head, I cover my ears further,

and lie down. Every time I feel like I'm dozing off, another shriek or shout wakes me. Two o'clock. Two-thirty. I moan in frustration.

The voices dim and I peek outside. The fire has burned down to embers and I can't really make out how many people are still up and about in the dim light, but the good news is that they've quieted down. Relieved, I glance once more at the time and settle back into bed. A quarter past three. I'll certainly sleep in tomorrow – no getting up at 6:30 or 7:00 for me!

"F*** you!"

Shooting straight up out of bed, I gasp at the bellowing coming from just outside my window. A man and woman exchange belligerent curses at the top of their lungs, while another man's voice urges them to cool it. Frustrated as the barrage of insults grows even louder, the referee changes tactics and attempts to out-shout them with demands to "shut the (*Expletive deleted*) up!" In my internal thoughts, the foul language is expunged, but not in the vocabulary of my next door neighbors.

If F-bombs were real, this entire campground would have been decimated by now. I wrap another shirt around my head, trying to escape the verbal barrage.

There's a lull in the battle and I try to focus on slowing my breathing and relaxing my body, one bit at a time. Release the tension in my toes. Now my calves. Ahhhh. I keep going, the adrenaline no longer raging through my system.

F-Boom – the furious couple resume their limited-vocabulary screaming match.

This cycle continues for another hour until the assault comes to an abrupt halt. Silence. Then very quiet voices, which I can barely hear. Curious, I peek outside. The flashing blue and red lights atop a vehicle parked in front of their campsite brings a smile of relief to my face. I don't know how somebody got a phone signal, but obviously someone managed to call the cops. At four in the morning. I collapse back into my bed, pull off the extra padding around my ears, and drop off to sleep.

Being a creature of habit, I wake up at 6:35 and can't fall asleep again, so I get up and dress. By the time I return from a quick trip to the ladies' room, I discover two camp staff people standing watch over the hungover and sleep-deprived (aww!) folks in the site next door as they pack up their belongings and eventually clear out of camp. Having seen that I'm up and about, the camp hosts come tap on my door.

"We're so sorry about last night," the man says, shaking his head. "We're hearing from people all over the camp who heard the noise, but I imagine it was particularly bad for the immediate neighbors." He hands me a piece of paper showing a map of the campground with one of the "private residence" buildings circled. "If you have any emergency after office hours, you just come ring the bell here and let us know."

The woman adds, "We've got a landline in the house and didn't realize that folks can't always get cell coverage in camp, especially in this loop. We're getting someone in here this coming week to see if we can do something about that."

"Again, we're really sorry about the disturbance," the man adds. "We're looking at some new rules about group sizes to avoid this kind of problem in the future."

"I appreciate that," I say, hoping they can fix the phone coverage issue, since I still wouldn't have felt comfortable walking out to their house in the middle of the night to report the problem.

"We're inviting everyone to join us for coffee and pastries," the woman says. "Come on down to the office. *Unlimited* coffee," she adds, nodding knowingly.

"That sounds great. I'm on my way." I think I'll need about a gallon this morning if I'm going to make it through the day.

Chapter 17

"She got it! The loan came through!"

Lisa sounds ecstatic and I'm thrilled. "That's great news! I'm so happy for her. Tell her I hope she has a wonderful experience in college. It'll be a lot of hard work, but she should also take time to enjoy making new friends and having fun."

"I'll sure tell her that. I'm so glad both my kids will have this opportunity to get a college degree. When I think of how that woulda changed *my* life ... well, no use cryin' over spilt milk."

Reminded of a question that's been bothering me, I decide to go ahead and ask, since she brought up the topic. "You mentioned that you didn't go to college. Was that something you wanted to do at the time?"

She pauses before answering. "Yeah, I wanted to go, but we couldn't afford it and my grades weren't all that great. So," she says with a sigh, "you mighta guessed already, but my parents didn't have a whole lotta money by the time I was finishin' high school. Pop had developed this weird eye thing where he couldn't see very good. Like, he couldn't drive anymore or read or nothin'. So he was out of work and Mama had to cut back on her hours so she could help him out."

How awful! "I'm so sorry to hear that. How old were you when that happened?"

"Oh, well, I don't remember exactly. I mean, he went kinda blind over time, like it took maybe two years? So, I guess I was about … eleven? I'm not sure. Anyways, we didn't have much money after that, so I got a job waitressin' instead of goin' to college. But that's okay. Really. I mean, my parents did their best and it just is what it is. I ain't one to gripe about how things worked out."

My imagination is running wild with scenes of Lisa as a child living with me and Franklin. We were never what I'd call rich, but we were financially sound and certainly could have found a way to enable her to attend college. I'm thinking she might have done better in school if there hadn't been the difficulties at home. Surely the stress of her father losing his sight had an effect on her as a child. I picture her helping her Pop when she got home from school each afternoon, instead of doing her homework or going out to play with her friends.

I shake off my feelings of guilt. Yes, by the time Franklin and I had been married several years, we had the means to care for a child in the manner I'm imagining. But Lisa would have been approaching her teens by that time. At age sixteen, I couldn't have offered my newborn baby anywhere near that level of financial or emotional stability.

We chat for a bit longer about Emily's future and I ask about Michael. "Oh, that boy. Nothin' much ever new with him. He just buries himself in his work and I can't ever understand a thing he tells me about all that high tech stuff he does."

"Does he have a girlfriend?" I ask as I doodle stick figures on the back of a small pad of paper. I start drawing lines to join the little people in a sort of tangled family tree. Actually, it more resembles a spider web.

"If he does, he hasn't told me about her," she says,

chuckling. "She'd have to be real brainy to hang out with Michael. He's, like, married to his computers and chips and whatnot."

Before I can ask more questions about my grandson, Lisa declares that she's got to go. As always, I'm disappointed to not have hours to talk more, but I understand that she has a very busy life as a single mom working more than full-time. We sign off with her promising to send me photos of herself and the kids.

"I'll get them to you tonight," she says before ending the call.

"I can hardly wait!"

***

Just as I'm finishing washing up the dishes after dinner and seriously considering going to bed by eight o'clock, my cellphone starts announcing incoming messages with a series of *pings*. I quickly dry my hands and grab the device, tapping on the first notification to open the app. Photos!

Lisa has sent a series of shots of her daughter at different ages. Here she is in a kitty costume, I assume for Halloween. Emily appears to be about five or six. She's smiling broadly and her two front teeth are missing. It's adorable! In another photo, she's a few years older and wearing a pink dress with a matching pink ribbon in her dark hair. The next shot shows her all bundled up in a parka, knit cap, and ski goggles, her mouth wide open (Screaming? Laughing?) as she slides down a snowy hill on a sled. In the final picture, I tear up as I see that she's turned into a pretty young woman in a cap and gown, smiling triumphantly as she grasps a scroll tied in green and white ribbons that match her graduation attire.

Michael's photos include one of him as a toddler in teddy bear pajamas, complete with a hood with fuzzy ears; another with him posing with a hockey stick in full uniform; a very serious boy of about 12 or 13 wearing a blue tie and dark jacket, with hints of other people on either side of him but cropped out of the shot; and a close-up, artsy profile of my grandson as a young adult, gazing off into the distance.

I wait for more pictures to come through of Lisa, but my phone remains silent. I send her a message thanking her for all the wonderful shots, but decide not to nag her for ones of herself. I'll wait and bring it up again next time we talk.

Dying to share my new treasures with someone, I text Ruth to see if she's up for some company. When she comes back with a "thumbs-up" emoji, I throw on a sweatshirt, grab my phone and headlamp, and practically skip over to her place, my earlier exhaustion forgotten.

Ruth fawns over the pictures with *Isn't that adorable* and *Quite the little man*, nodding with approval at each shot. I've downloaded the only decent photo of Lisa that I found on her Facebook page, and Ruth examines that one carefully.

"I'm thinking she has my smile," I offer.

Ruth purses her lips and studies the picture for a moment before nodding. "Yes, I think I can see that. And your coloring, too. Do you still have that photo of you and Franklin with your folks? Your hair was about that same shade of brown, wasn't it?"

I brush back a strand of my gray hair as I think back on when that shot was taken. During the bad period after Franklin disappeared from my life, I purged nearly all of my photos that included him. Fortunately, I held on to a few that contained other people who were important to me. Now that my parents have passed away, that picture from Dad's retirement party is something I cherish.

"Are you making any plans to meet your family in person?" she asks, bringing me back to the present.

I explain that I've brought up the idea a few times, but with Lisa's unforgiving work schedule and the kids' busy lives, it's been hard to find a time when that might happen. "I'm hoping we can work something out around Christmas or New Year's. Now, I'll admit that traveling to New Jersey in the winter doesn't sound terribly appealing, but if the timing can work out, maybe I can fly Lisa and even the kids out to Phoenix or someplace warm for a vacation."

Her eyes widen. "Wow. That sounds exciting but also pretty expensive. I know things are going better for you now in that department, but ... can you really afford that? And you might want to consider that some families don't necessarily get along all that well. Maybe ..."

I cut her off. "I thought you'd be more encouraging, Ruth. Look at *your* family – you're always on cloud nine when you get together with your daughters. Or ... or ... what about your grandson, Gabe? How can you talk about not helping your grandchildren afford to spend time with you? Have you forgotten that we'll be vacationing with Gabe and Ethan just a few weeks from now? Don't tell me you're going to ask them to pay you back for their campground reservations and their tickets for the boat tour."

Her eyes moisten with unshed tears. "Ellie, dear, I didn't mean to shoot you down. I was just concerned about your financial situation. I'm sorry if I overstepped."

Embarrassed at my outburst, I apologize for overreacting. "I really should get to bed. With all that commotion last night, I only got about three hours of sleep."

She opens her arms wide for a hug. "I understand completely. If those people had been camped close to me last night, I'd probably have been in bed tonight before suppertime."

Relieved that we aren't ending the evening on a sour note, I return to my place, thinking about what Ruth said earlier. I know she meant well, but it seems like she doesn't consider my newly-discovered family to be quite as *genuine* as her own family. In a way, I suppose that's true, but with no other close relatives still alive, it feels really good to have discovered Lisa and the kids. I want to nurture our connection. They are my family.

Chapter 18

Moving to a new location is always exciting. After three weeks of exploring the area around Crater Lake, I'm off to stay just a few nights near Mount Hood while Ruth meets up with some old friends of hers who live in Bend, Oregon. I'm excited to see this majestic mountain, and to treat myself to spending one night at the gorgeous lodge at the base of its ski area.

Once I've set up my camper at the lower elevation campground, I drive up the winding road to the historic lodge well up the flanks of the volcanic mountain. All along my drive today, I've caught glimpses of the peak, surprised to see all the swaths of snow still striping its slopes in August. When I reach the end of the road, I'm delighted to see the magnificent hotel perched beneath the steep slope of the peak. Stone walls and dramatically pitched rooflines lead my eyes up to the impossibly blue skies. I feel like I've been transported to the Swiss Alps. I step out of my Jeep and feel the cool, crisp high mountain air.

Inside the lodge, more stonework and hefty wooden beams continue the alpine feel of the place. I check in and make my way to my room, passing oversized windows offering views of the mountains surrounding this area. Gorgeous! When I swing open the door to my abode for the night, I'm greeted with the rich hue of wooden floors, wooden bed frames, and even wood paneling on the walls. I feel like the room is offering me a warm, welcoming hug.

After a lovely dinner in one of the lodge restaurants, I sit outside for a bit, wrapped in an oversized sweater, marveling at the layers of sunset colors painting the sky and the peaks along the horizon. When I become chilled, I change into my swim suit and head to the hot tub, star-gazing through the steam rising from the water. Even with the spa-produced fog, the view of the sky is awe-inspiring. Compared to what can be seen at lower elevations or in campgrounds close to a city, there are an amazing number of visible stars, and the Milky Way forms an ethereal arc across the firmament. Only three other people share the hot pool with me, and everyone seems content to enjoy the soak in silence. Finally, I retreat to my cozy nest and read in bed until I find myself dozing off.

In the morning, a pair of ladies who were out on the deck with me at sunset last night invite me to join them at breakfast. Although I've enjoyed the peace and quiet of being on my own, it's quite enjoyable to have someone to talk to as well. It turns out that Nancy and Eva are sisters, both currently single. They get together once a year for a week of travel and relaxation.

"Last autumn we drove along the Blue Ridge Parkway to see the changing leaves," Eva tells me. "It was spectacular!"

Nancy pulls out her phone and offers up proof. "I'll have to add that to my list," I say, wondering if Lisa and the kids have ever been there in the fall. Are the trees as pretty up north in New Jersey? Maybe we can meet up this October somewhere close enough for them to take off for a few days. I don't know if I can wait until Christmas to meet them in person.

I share photos of some of my travels in the southwest, then segue into showing off my new-found family, without getting into any details about our somewhat unusual situation.

Eva turns the conversation back to traveling destinations and we end up exchanging email addresses and promises to keep in touch. I've learned over the past few years of traveling that it'll be unlikely that our paths will cross again, but you never know for sure. No matter what, I've enjoyed spending time with the sisters.

After a final visit to an outdoor patio with marvelous views, I pack up and walk out toward the parking lot, passing by three young men removing climbing harnesses and helmets, sizable backpacks strewn on the ground behind their vehicle.

Curious, I ask, "Did you climb to the top of the mountain?"

The burliest fellow replies. "That was our plan, but there's too much danger of rock fall towards the top. Abe almost got taken out by one!" he says, pointing to one of his companions.

Abe shrugs, like it was no big deal. "I want to come back next May and give it another shot. This'll be my 47th highpoint."

"Highpoint?" I say, wondering if that means he's climbed exactly 46 mountains before today. Or if he considers this a particularly spectacular peak, thus a high point of his visit.

Abe replies, "You know, like the spot at the highest elevation in each of the fifty states. Mount Hood is the tallest mountain in Oregon, making it the highpoint of the state. So, Paul has done only eighteen," he explains, pointing to the burly guy, "but that includes most of the western states, so he's ticking off the hard ones first."

The third man speaks up. "I'm the newbie. Just six highpoints, but I do get out and hike a lot. These maniacs talked me into coming."

I know that Mount Elbert in my native Colorado is the highest peak there. And Mount Whitney is the tallest in California, where I lived for quite a while. But what about states with no mountains, like Kansas or Florida or Nebraska? With a count of 46 states already, Abe must be including some of the flat states.

"Does Florida *have* a highpoint?" I ask, wondering if he took the elevator to the top floor of the tallest Miami skyscraper.

He chuckles. "Sure. Only it's just 345 feet above sea level in a little park, just to the right of the restroom. It's hard to even tell that it's higher than the land around it, but somebody must have surveyed the land and worked that out."

"That's quite a creative hobby you fellows have come up with," I say.

Abe shakes his head. "We're far from being the first highpointers. There are thousands of members of a Highpointers Club, and probably thousands more who just travel around the country climbing highpoints who never heard of the club. Besides the state highpoints, people go after county highpoints, National Park highpoints —"

Paul interrupts, laughing. "—the highest Walmart in each state."

The third man, who's been focusing on loading gear into the car, steps closer and adds, "Or other lists that don't involve altitude, like visiting all the brewpubs in a state. That's my hobby. The great thing about it, besides sampling some great beer, is that the list is constantly changing, so I'll probably never finish!" He high-fives Paul.

"We failed on Mount Hood," Abe says, holding his hand up to slap as well, "so we need to make up for it with breweries today. What say you, boys?"

"Brew pub, brew pub, brew pub," they all chant.

With that, they climb into their car and wave as they depart.

A minute later, I follow them out of the lot, driving back down the mountain to my campground. "I'm home," I say to my little camper when I step inside. "Did you think I'd abandoned you last night?"

Yes, I realize it's a bit peculiar to talk to an inanimate object, but who's going to know besides me?

I enjoy a short hike through the woods, but head back to camp early as the weather starts to change. Although the temperature was quite pleasant when I set out, the wind has picked up and it's turned much cooler. That'll teach me to check the forecast beforehand – my light wind jacket isn't nearly warm enough to keep me comfortable. I imagine it's turned downright cold higher up the mountain at the lodge. By the time I finish dinner, the air has chilled even more and the forecast says it might dip below freezing tonight. September is right around the corner, and Mother Nature is reminding us that summer won't last forever.

Before crawling into bed, I retrieve my extra blanket from its storage spot and switch on the furnace I haven't needed for the past several months, setting the thermostat to 55 degrees. It'll probably wake me if it does come on during the night, but I hate trying to sleep if I'm cold.

The noisy furnace fan does rouse me at one point, but I simply roll over and fall asleep again quickly, becoming used to the sound. Dreaming of shivering in an overly air conditioned restaurant while dressed in shorts and a tank top, I come awake again. My nose feels numb with the cold. I hear the loud rumble of the heater, so why am I freezing?

Reaching over to the thermostat, I slide the temperature setting to a much higher point, then lie back in bed. After a minute or so, I roll over and hold my hand near the blower. Cold air chills my already-frigid fingers. What's going on? I roll out of bed and push the knob to its warmest position, then wrap my blanket around me as I wait for the heat. Brrr – the air is still blowing cold.

Then it occurs to me that I might be out of propane. No propane, no heat. Damn. It's three in the morning and I've got a choice of turning off the furnace fan and freezing for the rest of the night, or going outside and checking to see why the system didn't switch over to my backup propane tank. I pull back a curtain to check the outdoor thermometer I've stuck to the window with a suction cup. Thirty one degrees! Brrr!

Biting the proverbial bullet, I yank on a pair of pants under my nightgown, slip my bare feet into my ice cold sneakers, and dig out my warm coat. Headlamp shining brightly with new batteries, I hurry outside and uncover the twin propane tanks. Aha. I never turned on the backup tank. Chilling my hands further by adjusting the metal knobs, I get everything reset the way I should have when I first set up camp, decide to mess with the cover in the morning, and scurry back inside.

Flipping the furnace switch back on, I cuss when my legs are hit with cold air again. Now what? But after a few more seconds, I hear the gas burner *whoosh* to life and remember that it always takes a little bit of time for the system to heat up. Soon, a lovely blast of hot air is streaming out and I quickly remove my excess clothes and dive into bed, still shivering from my venture outside. Next thing I know, I open my eyes and realize that it's growing light outside. The furnace is chugging away and the room is toasty to the point of being a bit too warm. I guess I never turned the thermostat back down.

Okay, number one on my must-do list is Refill propane tank. Number two is Make sure both tanks are turned on. Number three is Pay more attention to what I'm doing.

Bundled up against the chill of morning, I make my way to the restroom. When I returned to camp yesterday, I had noticed a hammock strung between two trees in the site across from mine. The young man preparing dinner on a camp stove seemed to be traveling alone, other than having a small, black dog as his companion. The last I noticed before retiring for the night, he didn't seem to have anyplace to actually sleep. No tent and a compact sedan that wouldn't offer much space for his lanky frame.

This morning, the hammock appears to have a tent-like

cover over it and, judging by the way it is bulging at the bottom, someone is inside. Surely he didn't spend the night suspended above the ground in sub-freezing temperatures! When I step inside the ladies room, two girls of about eighteen are huddled beside the hand dryer, pressing its power button each time the warm air turns off. That brings back memories of my earliest camping experience, before I bought my A-frame camper and was trying to sleep in the back of my Jeep with inadequate bedding. At least the girls haven't had to resort to wearing underwear on their heads for warmth, as I did. I snort in amusement at the memory. Fortunately, the hand dryer is making too much noise for the girls to hear me and wonder why some old lady is laughing to herself in a toilet stall.

I consider suggesting that they put something on their feet other than flip-flops, but maybe that's all they have along on their camping trip. Instead of jackets, they each seem to have on two or three layers of tops and they're wearing colorful pajama bottoms. I'm wrapped in my winter parka, heavy jeans, warm socks, and sneakers. No wonder they're cold.

As I return to my camper, there is activity from the hammock. Long legs appear and the little dog pops out, followed by its owner, rubbing his eyes and running a hand through his tangled hair.

"Did you sleep out here all night?" I ask, my hands dug deep into my coat pockets for warmth.

"Yeah. I always sleep in my hammock." He grins, spreads his arms wide and stretches. "It's great!"

"You weren't cold?"

"Nope. Buster and I keep plenty warm."

I step inside my comfy trailer and wonder if he just adds more dogs as the temperature drops. Thirty degrees, apparently, is merely a one dog night. Maybe at fifteen degrees, he needs two dogs, and when the temperature drops to zero, that's a three dog night. Now my brain starts playing "Old Fashioned Love Song" on repeat. Three Dog Night wasn't a band I followed much back in the day, but now I expect I'll hear them in my head for hours.

But for now, there's a long scenic driving loop I'd like to tackle, so it's time to hit the road *(...to Shambala)*.

Chapter 19

Ruth and I greet each other as if we've been apart for ages. Although I enjoyed myself on my lone travels in the Mount Hood area, I missed her energy and enthusiasm to inspire me to seek out more adventures and to reach out to others. She's such a social person. I'm much more on the shy side.

Our focus this week will be in and around Olympic National Park. Once settled in at our new campground, where our sites are side-by-side, we hop into my car and set off toward the Hoh Rain Forest to hike and enjoy the hot springs. Once again, we find ourselves driving along a road through dense forest, but the humidity and lushness of the greenery is noticeably different from the areas we've visited over the past month or so.

As I round a curve, I brake quickly. Just ahead, blocking the road, are five large animals – elk. One turns toward us and I realize there are two much smaller elk just behind her. "Look at the babies!" Ruth says.

Apparently satisfied that my Jeep poses no immediate threat, the elk cow strolls toward a couple of other adults and the two calves follow, one attempting to suckle as mom keeps moving. The youngsters share the large animals' coloring of beige rumps, light brown bodies, and darker necks, but one also has light polka dots along its sides.

As we watch, more critters emerge from the forest and meander across the road. The cows are huge – easily five or six hundred pounds each would be my guess. More calves follow their mothers onto the pavement, two frolicking on their long, spindly legs.

With a couple of cars stopped behind us, and one more waiting in the opposite direction, I wonder if I should try easing forward to encourage the herd – we've counted eighteen animals so far – to leave the roadway. Before I make up my mind, the sedan coming toward us begins creeping forward, the driver slapping his door and calling out to the elk, "Okay, ladies. Time to head back into the woods." Unperturbed, a few cows stare at him as if to say, "We'll go when we feel like it," but most of the group eases across the road, babies close behind. Once our lane is cleared of animals, I roll forward cautiously, keeping an eye out for anyone changing direction or for new arrivals from my right. Shortly, all of the elk have disappeared from sight.

"Wasn't that wonderful!" Ruth says, stowing away her cell phone. Between us, I'll bet we snapped a hundred photos of our wild visitors.

Continuing on to the visitor center, we opt to hike first, then soak in the hot spring pool. The trail is unlike any other I've experienced. Ferns sprout everywhere, and the trees are incredibly tall, with mosses growing on their trunks and dangling in long, thick strands from their branches. Wrapped in our rain coats, we can't tell if it is currently raining or if all the moisture dripping from the lush vegetation is from a recent rainfall. A fan of fern leaves sparkles with drops of water. I've never seen so much green and so much moisture!

After crossing numerous tiny creeks, using our trekking poles to keep from slipping on the moss-covered stones, we come to an amazing triple waterfall. A high foot bridge constructed from massive wooden beams offers passage above a deep crevice. The stream flows at a level equal to the elevation of the bridge, then plunges fifty feet or more through three rocky fissures into the narrow canyon below us. Spectacular!

We return to the trailhead amidst the delightfully rich smells of wet spruce and rotting leaves, ready for a warming soak in the hot springs.

Although there is a lovely place we could soak that is part of a resort, we decide to locate a more rustic and lesser-known mineral hot springs that we learned about from a couple of women we encountered on our hike today. Unable to locate it in my car's GPS system, I have Ruth read me the directions they jotted down for us.

"After about a mile, turn left on unpaved road with old signpost," she says.

I slow to a crawl when we've driven three quarters of a mile and we both stare at the left side of the road, searching for our turn.

"That could be it," Ruth says, pointing. The track she's spotted appears to be slightly overgrown, but as much rain as they get around here, I'll bet things grow back virtually overnight. It seems like a possible route. At the intersection, there's a weathered wooden post with two rusty bolts sticking out of it, which might qualify as an old signpost.

"I'll give it a try," I say, making the turn. "What's next?"

She clears her throat. "After about another mile, take right fork."

After a mile and a half, I'm starting to doubt that we're on the right route, but we decide to push on just a bit farther. At two miles, just when we decide to look for a place to turn around, I spot a fork in the road ahead. I swing to the right and we both let out a cheer as a small building comes into view with a faded sign saying *Back of Beyond Hot Springs*. We park beside one other car in the small lot.

Inside, a woman with an extremely lengthy gray braid trailing down her back greets us. She's wearing a long, flowing robe of many shades of purple, blue, green, and yellow; about a dozen beaded bracelets in a rainbow of colors; and silver rings of various shapes on all ten fingers.

"Welcome to Back of Beyond," she says in a quiet, melodious voice. "My name is Venus. Have you visited us before?"

"No, we haven't," I say, noticing that Ruth seems mesmerized by her colorful garb. Ruth adores bright colors. Her own hunter orange shirt, however, seems subdued in comparison to the lady's attire.

Venus explains that they have five separate *water sanctuaries*, each situated in a natural setting in the woods along the hot spring, offering bamboo privacy fences so visitors may soak in the mineral waters *au naturel*. "We ask that you do not wear any sort of clothing in the waters, so that we can preserve its natural state," she says. "Within your sanctuary, you will find an open air shower. Please rinse before stepping into the hot spring to remove any soap or shampoo residue, body lotions, or deodorant."

Nude? We'll be soaking in the woods in the *altogether*? I glance at Ruth, who is smiling and nodding as she listens to Venus's explanation. Oh, well. If she can do it, so can I. Assuming the "privacy fence" matches my definition of *privacy*.

"You'll be in the Shiva water sanctuary," she tells us. "Continue driving down the road another quarter mile and you'll see a sign pointing you to the parking spots for Shiva and Vishnu. That will put you only a very short walk from your sanctuary."

Following her directions, I move the car to the new parking space. Unless somebody walked here from the office, we seem to have this nook of the woods to ourselves – there aren't any other cars. "I want to check this out first," I say, eyeing the two marked trails leading from the parking area. Just how far apart are these "private sanctuaries"?

Ruth follows me down the Shiva trail where we encounter the fenced-off portion of the hot spring. The fence is roughly five feet high, adequate to hide all but a portion of my head if I stand behind it. As long as nobody approaches too closely, they shouldn't be able to see beyond it. We circle around and discover that the fence consists of four sides of a hexagon – the missing two sides offer an open view in the opposite direction of where we parked.

"So, someone could just walk past us on this side." I frown.

"I like that it's not entirely enclosed," Ruth says. "Nobody's going to see us. Look how dense the forest is. They'd have to be following the Shiva path to get back here. Anyway, nobody else seems to be around."

"Okay," I say, giving in. "Let's get our stuff."

We walk back to my SUV and rearrange the tote bags we've both brought along, leaving behind our swim suits and sunscreen. Returning to the enclosure, Ruth begins to strip immediately. There isn't a great deal of dry land to stand on, but I find a spot, turn my back, and disrobe as well, holding my towel close and wrapping it around me as soon as possible. I stuff my clothes into my tote, then look around for a good place to leave it. Ruth has simply set hers on the ground and is already rinsing off in the shower. I divert my eyes and set my tote beside hers. She drapes her towel over the fence and wades into the hot water, moaning with pleasure as she eases herself down so only her head bobs above the surface.

"It's heavenly!" she declares. "Hurry up and shower so you can get in!"

Self-conscious, I rinse quickly, flip my towel over the fence beside hers, and slosh into the steaming water, lowering myself in as quickly as possible.

"Oooh, this is wonderful," I say.

"Ommm," she answers, raising both hands just to the surface of the water and holding them in the classic meditation position.

I tilt my head back and gaze at the shapes of the tree limbs above us, silhouetted against the sky. Steam circles above, giving the scene a dreamy, other-worldly presence. When we get a bit overheated, we move back toward the shore and sit with only our legs in the water. I've grown comfortable with being here in the buff with my dearest friend.

A breeze swirls the steam and I'm hypnotized by the new patterns. The wind gusts and my exposed skin feels a chill, so I slip back into the deep part of the hot spring.

"Look how cloudy it's become," I say, squinting up through the mist and realizing I can't find any blue sky above us now. The breeze picks up again, blowing more steadily.

"I think it's starting to rain. We should probably head out," Ruth says.

Moments later, the skies open up – it's pouring! We stagger out of the toasty water just as a strong gust blasts us. It snatches our towels and they sail into the water before we can grab them.

"I'll get the towels. Make sure our clothes don't blow in!" Ruth says.

Although both totes have tipped over, I'm able to snatch them before they can take off. The wind is whistling through the trees, cold rain is bombarding us, our towels are sopping wet, and I'm pretty sure our clothes are already damp from the rain. They'll be soaked by the time we get dressed in this downpour.

"What should we do?"

"Bring the totes and run!" she answers, already dashing out of the enclosure buck naked, both soggy towels tucked under one arm.

Cold and starting to shiver, I clutch the totes to my chest with both arms and run to catch up.

"Keys!" she hollers, yanking on the handle to the passenger side.

"Shit!" I drop both totes, then dig through mine until I finally locate my car keys in the bottom. Fortunately, the electronic device is still functioning, despite the rain. We jump inside, slam the doors, and I start the engine immediately, hoping to get heat as soon as possible.

Catching our breath, we look at each other and burst out laughing. Here we are, two older women, stark naked and muddy, sitting in a car looking like something the cat dragged in.

"Have you ever streaked before?" Ruth asks. "That was quite a fad back in the '70s, as I recall."

Me? Run around naked in a public place *on purpose*? "I never did, but some guy streaked my college graduation ceremony during the dean's speech. How about you?" I ask, being facetious.

"Only once," she says. "A popular local radio station dreamed up a competition between two rival colleges to see which one could boast the largest number of streakers in one night. David and I were curious and lived only five miles from one of the campuses, so we decided to go check it out.

"They were gathered in the football stadium and I'll bet there were at least a couple thousand people there. Most were already naked when we arrived, and just running around laughing and singing, having the best old time! I was standing near one co-ed who was buck naked other than tennis shoes and a small pack she was stuffing with clothing – hers as well as her friends' clothes, it looked like. I asked her to convince me that it would be okay to strip and join everyone, seeing that David and I were at least ten years older than anyone we saw."

"And she talked you into it," I say, seeing where this is going.

122

"Or gave me that final nudge to allow myself to give it a go. David was less sure, but he wasn't going to stand there, fully dressed, while his wife ran around naked. Besides, by then we were almost the only ones with our clothes on, which made us feel self-conscious. So we both stripped. It was a blast!"

Oh, Ruth. You never cease to amaze me.

Once the car warms up, we don our damp pants and shirts, forgoing panties and bras for now. I turn the heater fan on high and we head back to our campground.

**

We fall back into our comfortable routine of alternating days of outdoor adventures with quieter days. Now that I'm putting more effort again into promoting my proofreading services, I generally spend four to six hours on our "off" days working on manuscripts that have been sent to me. I've also decided to make a concerted effort to keep in touch with people – old friends from my time living in California, people I've met while out camping and hiking, and my in-laws – Franklin's brother, Hank and his wife, Cheryl – who were so supportive during that period when Franklin staged his *Disappearing Act*, leaving not only his wife of nearly forty years, but also his only sibling without any explanation nor any way to contact him. Ah, but that's all water under the bridge now. Except that Hank deserves to hear from me far more often than a call on his birthday, a card at Christmas, and the rare photo or text message. I try to set aside some time once a week to compose a few emails or make a few phone calls.

And, of course, to reach out to Lisa with little tidbits of news about what I'm up to and prompts for updates about herself and my grandchildren.

Emily's classes just started this week and I'm anxious to hear how she's transitioned from high school to college. When Sunday afternoon finally arrives, I'm on pins and needles waiting for Lisa's usual phone call.

"She's had a very busy first week," Lisa reports. "She's real excited about her biology teacher and what they'll be studyin', but I'm thinkin' she's gonna have to drop that class."

When I ask why, Lisa hesitates. "So, the thing is that her books and materials for all her classes were a lot more expensive than we figured. If I had known how much all that would come to, we woulda asked for a bigger student loan. Even without the biology class, we've gone way over budget. I don't know how they can ask these kids to pay for all the stuff they're requirin' for the class! And it looks like *all* the science classes are like that — real expensive."

"I'm so sad to hear that, Lisa. I know you said Emily wants to major in some field of science. Isn't there another way for her to afford that class? Can any of the equipment or books be rented or bought used?"

She explains that they'd already tried that route, but the cost was still beyond their means.

It seems tragic to have gotten this far and have the girl's hopes shattered. I felt so proud when I heard that Emily is a science whiz — isn't there still a big gender gap when it comes to science and technology? She deserves a chance to pursue her true interests.

"How much money are we talking about here?" I ask, doing some mental calculations. I'm expecting payment this coming week for my last proofreading project and I'll receive an annuity deposit on the 15th of the month.

"Oh, Mom. If you're thinkin' of sending us more money for Emily's education, I can't let you do that. You've already done so much for her!"

I press on. "How much?"

With a sigh, she reveals that her daughter needs to purchase eight hundred dollars' worth of textbooks and equipment. "But she'll be able to keep usin' most of the supplies in future classes, so it won't be as much next semester."

After several more protests on her part about my sending more money, I insist on covering the cost. Lisa was almost in tears when we signed off. After thinking about it a bit longer, I decide to wire an even $1,000 to her, in case some additional expenses arise.

I wasn't there for my daughter all these years, but at least I can help my granddaughter have an opportunity to follow her dream. I remind myself to ask more about Michael. I hope he doesn't feel slighted by all the attention I've given to his sister. I want to learn more about *his* hopes, get a chance to talk by phone, get a sense of what he's like.

I'm turning into a regular social butterfly!

Chapter 20

As we explore the Pacific Northwest, we're astounded at the variation in climate and scenery. After spending a week exploring Olympic National Park and the coastline, we plan our move further north and inland in Washington to the wonders of the North Cascade mountains and the national park bearing their name. We'll be "boondocking" at our park campground nested in the forest – no electricity or water hook-ups to our campers. I fill up my trailer's water storage tanks before driving to our more "primitive" site. My portable solar panel will be put to good use for the next ten days, assuming I can get a spot that receives some direct sunlight through the trees.

Anticipating that we'll encounter long delays and expensive tolls, we choose a driving itinerary that avoids ferry crossings, even though it's a much more circuitous route. It'll be a long day on the road, albeit a scenic one. After crawling through the Seattle area in bumper-to-bumper traffic, we finally exit the interstate to a minor, two-lane highway. I pull off and stop as soon as I find a safe spot where we both can park and take a break.

"That was tedious," Ruth says as she stretches both arms high above her head, then leans over to each side. "I thought we'd have to set up camp right there on the interstate."

I glance at my watch. With about another hour and a half to go, we should reach our destination around 6 P.M. That sounds perfect – I'm already starting to feel slightly hungry, so I'll definitely be ready for dinner when we arrive. "Traffic seems reasonably light here. I think it'll be smooth sailing the rest of the way," I say.

Once we've gotten some of the kinks out of our bodies, we climb back into our vehicles and set out again. There are a smattering of homes along the route, plenty of trees, some open meadows, and a classic red barn now and then. Bridges escort us over creeks and rivers while distant mountains peek at us through the trees as we round a curve in the road. It's a lovely, peaceful area, so refreshing after the congestion of the big city.

Brake lights ahead warn me to slow, then creep to a halt behind a long line of cars and trucks. It dawns on me that I haven't seen any traffic coming toward me in a while, so maybe there's construction ahead and they've got both directions stopped for a bit. I turn off my engine and switch on the radio, then search for a classical music station. I'll just relax while we wait. Ruth walks past and waves back at me as she continues forward along the line of stopped vehicles. She stops now and then to chat with other drivers standing beside their cars.

Fifteen minutes later, Ruth is back. "Bad news," she says. "There's been an accident about a quarter mile ahead, and there's a jackknifed semi blocking the entire highway, plus two really messed up passenger cars. An ambulance arrived a little while ago, but it looks like the big tow trucks haven't even arrived yet to start working on clearing the road."

"Oh dear. Are they setting up a detour?" I've noticed a couple of passenger cars heading the opposite direction, but I watched as a small hatchback in line just ahead of me decided to give up and head back the way we came. That required a three-point turn on his part, something that would be impossible for us with our trailers.

"Nothing that helps us. We may as well just get comfortable. It could be an hour, maybe two."

"Rats."

"I'm going to walk back and see how long the line is," she says, and sets off again. For a while, I can see her in my side extension mirror, playing the part of the town crier, spreading the news and collecting more information as she stops to visit with people in the cars stopped behind us.

A half hour ticks by, then another. Ruth goes on another reconnaissance mission and reports back that the big rig is almost ready to be moved, but it could be yet another hour before they get it out of the way and clean up the debris from the wreck.

It's already half past six and we're about forty-five minutes from our destination in normal traffic. "I'm famished. Do you have anything handy I could snack on?" Digging food out of my folded-up trailer involves crawling around in a dark "cave" that's about three feet tall and dragging things out the bottom of the half door. With her more conventional camper, she'll be able to walk upright and move around to access everything in her kitchen area.

"I'm hungry, too. I've been thinking about those hamburger patties we bought and my mouth keeps watering. You know, I'll bet I could cook a couple of those up while we wait."

"I could slice a tomato and some onion."

"We've got lettuce, fresh rolls, and spicy brown mustard. I think we're all set!"

It's a bit more cramped than when Ruth is set up in a campground with the slide-outs opening up more living space, but compared to my place, there's plenty of room for both of us to prepare the burgers. Ruth pulls off a bit of the meat and takes it to Charli, who isn't terribly happy to be waiting in her truck with nobody to pay attention to her.

We take our hamburgers outside and flip open the back hatch on my Jeep, using that area as a table while we eat standing up.

"That smells delicious," a man says, stopping by to lust after our dinners. "How much for an order of two burgers?"

He's joking, I hope.

Still, Ruth darts back inside and emerges with a stack of small paper plates, a large bag of tortilla chips, and a jar of salsa. Soon, we're hosting a tailgate party for the folks parked around us. Somebody brings a six-pack of colas, another contributes an enormous jar of peanuts, and others pass around homemade cookies and strips of beef jerky.

"We're moving!" somebody shouts, and the party quickly disperses as people scurry back to their cars. Ruth locks up her camper and we both hop into our towing vehicles, ready to continue our journey at last.

***

The campground is spacious, with plenty of room between sites. Gazing out my camper windows, if I choose the right angle I can pretend there's no one else around me in the forest. The only drawback is that it's about a three minute walk each way to the nearest bathroom. Now, that may not seem like much, but sometimes when nature calls, three minutes can seem like forever. But on a positive note, given my bladder's reaction to a couple of cups of coffee in the morning, I know I'll get plenty of walking in even on our "rest" days.

Ruth has selected an ambitious hike for us today: Cascade Pass. According to the information she downloaded, we'll be gaining 1,700 feet in elevation on a trail that's slightly less than 4 miles in length. And, of course, then we'll be dropping back down those same distances to return to our vehicle.

"I'm not sure I can hike something that steep," I tell her. While the total length of the trail is within the range of what I've hiked in the past, the climb sounds daunting. I've rarely gained more than 1,000 feet on any outing.

"We won't know until we try," she says. "Even the first part of the hike sounds gorgeous, so I think we should give it a shot."

So, we're off to tackle another adventure.

The drive to the trailhead is lengthy, winding, and quite lovely. We hardly encounter any other vehicles on the well-maintained gravel road and figure we've made a good decision to get an early start for what is described as a popular hike. Shortly before we reach our destination, according to my GPS, we're puzzled to see cars parked along the roadside.

"I wonder where those folks are hiking," Ruth says as we continue toward the parking lot for our trailhead.

Coming around one final curve, we realize that we are most definitely not the first to arrive this morning. The lot seems packed – but Ruth spots a narrow slot which I manage to squeeze my Jeep into after having her climb out of her side before I pull in. With difficulty, I slither out of the driver's side, pressing my door against the pickup beside me. I check that I didn't damage their truck, then side-step my way to the back of my car to retrieve my backpack and hiking sticks.

It's clear why this trail is so sought-after – the views are extraordinary! I've never seen the Swiss Alps in person, but the surrounding mountains resemble the photos I've seen. Steep, rugged, rocky peaks tower above cirques of snow. Trees and other greenery seem to flow down the lower slopes, leading the eye to verdant meadows below. As I peer into the distance, a progression of mountains march to the horizon, each appearing to be a deeper blue than the one before it.

"This is gorgeous!" I say, stopping to gape at the views and to take photos. We ascend switchback after switchback, gaining elevation steadily until I realize how high we've come in what seems like no time at all. Each leg of the trail offers more marvelous views as we pass a spot where the trees open up a bit, like a curtain opening to expose a postcard-perfect scene.

We munch on trail mix and sip water as we go, taking regular but very brief breaks. Finally, we arrive at the pass, which offers a series of long, flat stones for sitting and enjoying yet another new view of the valley beyond. A couple with two adorable daughters – ages seven and nine, we learn – scoots over to give us room to sit.

"Mommy! Mommy! Look!" the older one shouts, jumping to her feet and pointing toward a series of stone steps that lead to an outhouse. "What is it?"

This brings everyone to their feet. The child has spotted a white animal behind a bush, moving slowly and munching on leaves and grasses. The critter steps forward and a man announces, "Mountain goat."

Over the next half hour, four of the long-haired creatures wander out of the low shrubs and bushes to graze. Two tiny versions frolic around the adults, but are rounded up by the bigger animals when they stray too far. The kids' mother (we assume) often stops what she is doing and glares at the circle of humans taking photos. Her long, straight horns look like they could do some damage, so everyone keeps their distance. The adults all look pretty mangy, still shedding last winter's coats, while the kids look soft and very pet-able. I don't test out this observation.

The goats eventually disappear over a ridge and we decide to head back down the trail. Warned by hikers heading up, we keep watch for the bear they report having seen on the slopes between the trail switchbacks. We talk loudly and clatter our trekking poles together so we don't surprise the animal. When we arrive at the start of the trail, Ruth nudges me with her elbow.

"And you thought you couldn't hike that far!" she says with a wink.

I was having so much fun, I forgot to worry about the distance!

***

We stop off in a small town on the way back to camp to treat ourselves to homemade pie a la mode. After enjoying our treat, I step outside and call Lisa's number, excited to share my experiences from today. The call goes to voicemail.

Emily called to thank me for the money for her biology supplies shortly after I sent it, but since then I've only heard from my new-found family through text messages from Lisa. She's busier than ever and wasn't able to call me this past weekend. Now that I think about it, she's likely waiting tables tonight – I forgot about the time difference between the east coast and here. I remind myself not to let my expectations lead to disappointment. She's called most Sundays since we connected with each other, but that doesn't mean it's her duty to talk to me every week. I need to give her a little space.

In keeping with my goal to reach out to friends more regularly, I email a few photos from today to my old friends from my California days, Claire and Otis, and ask about their future travel plans. We keep saying we'd like to get together sometime, but haven't taken any action to make that happen. Maybe I can move us in that direction.

Chapter 21

"Grams!"

I feel a mixture of joy and longing as Ruth's grandson, Gabe, wraps his arms around her. How I dream of meeting my own grandchildren and being able to hug them! Gabe's partner, Ethan, offers me a warm hug before the two young men switch places and exchange hugs again with us two old ladies.

"You're early!" Ruth says. "I hope you boys didn't drive all night." I suppose, when you are in your 80s, males in their early 30s are still *boys*.

"Not *all* night," Gabe answers. "No worries, Grams. We took turn driving while the other guy slept."

Gabe is small, wiry, and quite outgoing, like his grandmother. Ethan is medium height, just a tad on the chunky side, and more reserved. They've been together for five years, and as far as I know from Ruth's stories, both of their families have been quite warm and accepting of their choice in partners.

"Thanks again for treating us to the boat tour, Grams," Ethan says. I love that he also calls her *Grams*.

She waves at him, dismissively. "My pleasure. I always look forward to our little adventures together, boys. Now, do you need help setting up your tent?"

They both laugh. "That's okay, Grams. We got this."

We've changed camps, once again, moving to just outside the south end of North Cascades National Park, near the town of Chelan. Ruth and I just arrived here late yesterday afternoon after a jaw-dropping drive over a high pass. The beauty of this region never ceases to amaze me! Our plan is to take a passenger ferry tomorrow from the south end of Lake Chelan to the north end, a distance of around 55 miles. We'll play tourist in and around the tiny town of Stehekin for several hours, then ferry back.

Ruth and I have teamed up to cook up a generous amount of spaghetti with meat sauce, a huge salad, and have purchased three flavors of ice cream, which are taking up almost all the space in her freezer. Gabe, again mimicking his grandmother, can consume seemingly limitless number of calories yet still stay slim. He loves ice cream.

After the boys are all set up in their camp (See? Now I've started calling them *boys*!) we gather around the picnic table in Ruth's place where we gorge ourselves. Gabe brings us up to date on how his job is going as manager of a hotel near Oakland, California.

"So, about a month ago we had a guest who asked us to lay out bath towels to cover the entire floor of his room. I thought maybe he was paranoid about the cleanliness of the carpet, so I offered to give him a room that we had just remodeled with new carpet, new bedding, the whole nine yards. Nope, that wouldn't do. He told me he could only sleep in a room with white floors."

"You're kidding!" Ruth says.

"True story. Then there was a couple who wanted one of our Jacuzzi suites, but they requested that we fill the tub with cold water, not hot, before they arrived."

"Because ...?" she asks.

"Because they wanted to keep their pet eel with them in the room. I asked if they needed any assistance in moving the eel from whatever-the-hell they use to hold it while they travel and get it up to their room, but they declined. All I know is that we wiped up a trail of water through the lobby, in the elevator, and down the hallway. None of the staff spotted anything unusual while they were transporting it. But Mary from housekeeping almost quit after going in to clean and discovering a 'snake' in the tub."

"Oh, my," Ruth says. "There's an image I won't forget!"

"The only eel I want to see is roasted and served in a sushi restaurant," I say.

Ruth and Gabe respond in stereo, "Yum – *unagi!*" while Ethan turns just slightly green.

We prompt Ethan about his work, but as an Information Technology guy, he knows we won't understand the details of the ins and outs of website development and security analysis. With a modest shrug, he says, "Our group grew to twenty people in the past year, which got unwieldy, so management reorganized the department and split us into two teams under our same original manager. So, they put me in charge of a team and gave me a fancy, new title, Manager of User Experience Solutions."

"That's a mouthful," I say.

"Or MUES for short," he adds.

Gabe chuckles and pipes in with *mew, mew, mew,* sounding like a cat. Ethan shakes his head, but is grinning. Charli stares at Gabe as if he's said something of great interest. Or maybe she's just hoping for a taste of eel.

***

We're on board the ferry early, on a brilliant morning with the lake water sparkling all around us. The craft moves at a good clip once it has left the more congested area of water whose shores are lined with homes and businesses of the town of Chelan. We spot two men on water jet skis criss-crossing behind our wake. Moving to the back of the ferry for a better view behind us, we realize that they are using the large, artificial waves created by our boat to launch their motorized water scooters high into the air with each pass. It's exciting to watch, but looks quite dangerous.

Ruth and I settle in some inside seats where we can get out of the wind, yet still enjoy the views of the shoreline and the forested peaks along the journey. The boys explore vantage points in the open air, but eventually come sit with us.

When we disembark at the north end of the long, skinny lake, we opt to rent bicycles and ride out to view an impressive waterfall that drops over three hundred feet. There is almost no traffic on the narrow, two-lane road, so we don't feel like we're about to be run over. A woman enjoying the falls with her family offers to take a group photo of us with the thundering water in the background. She probably wishes she hadn't – all four of us hand her our phones to take another shot.

On our way back, we reward ourselves by stopping at what may be the only place to grab a bite to eat. Fortunately, its popularity also owes credit to the delicious lunch items and mouth-watering desserts. We order another round of cookies to go for our long boat ride back to Chelan.

By the time we arrive at our campground, it's well past seven o'clock. Normally, we'd have finished dinner by now, but after eating all those goodies at lunch and on the ferry back, nobody is particularly hungry. Still, I pull out the remains of last night's salad and chop up some additional vegetables to add to it while Ruth bulks it up with more greens.

Just as we start cleaning up after eating, a man strolls past and pauses. "Didn't I see you all on the ferry today?" he asks.

I remember him. Full, longish hair heavily streaked with

gray – reminds me of my husband with his thick mane of white hair, only this guy isn't nearly as tall as Franklin. He's good-looking, with intensely blue eyes and a ready smile. He flashes it in my direction and I smile back.

Ruth answers, "Yep, we were there. Wasn't that a beautiful lake?!"

We exchange the usual small talk about where we all are from and how long we're staying. He introduces himself as Jon.

"So," he says, "are those your sons?"

I glance around and realize Ruth and the boys have scattered in several directions, back to clearing away our salad bowls and wiping down the tablecloth on the picnic table. "Oh, no, they're not mine – they're Ruth's. Her grandsons, I mean." Realizing that I'm stammering a bit, I don't try to clarify Gabe and Ethan's relationship.

"Do you have any kids?" he asks. I'm pretty sure he just checked out my left hand to see if I'm wearing a ring. I am not.

And here it is – my moment of truth. I've been anticipating this question since connecting with my daughter and now I can practice my new, honest reply. After decades of denying her existence and often following up with something like *it just wasn't in the cards*, I've finally decided to shed that ancient shame over my youthful indiscretion and just go with the truth.

"Yes, a daughter who lives in New Jersey," I say, standing up just a bit taller. "And two grandkids. How about you?"

There. That wasn't so hard, was it?

Al tells me about his two sons and five grandchildren. "When I lost my wife to breast cancer five years ago, I decided to retire a few years early and hit the road."

"Oh. Sorry to hear that." I pause, considering how I want to word this. "I lost my husband several years ago," I say, choosing not to elaborate. The word *lost* covers a lot of bases.

"So, we have the misfortune of sharing that in common," he says with a sigh. "Ah, but looking to the future, what are your plans while you're in this area? If you have an open evening, I'd like to invite you over for dinner."

"Wow. That's such a generous offer, Jon. But if we ..." I stop myself before I stick my foot in my mouth. I was about to insist that *we* – all four of us – bring some of the dishes, pot luck style if we joined him for dinner. But then it dawned on me that he was asking *me* to come to dinner. *I'd like to invite you*, singular, *over for dinner.*

Did he just ask me out on a date? Oh dear. I don't feel ready for anything like that. "Well, we only have this week to spend with the boys since they're both on vacation from work, so I ..." So I ... what? Fortunately, he fills in the gap in our conversation.

"I understand completely, Ellie. Tell you what. I'll be here through the end of the month, so if you'll be around after the guys leave and are still interested, I'm offering you a raincheck. Think about it and let me know."

"A raincheck, then." I try to give him a genuine smile. Maybe he's just being friendly and this isn't anything like a date.

"Great. I'd really like to get to know you better."

Okay. That sounds like a date.

"See you around, Ellie."

I sink onto the picnic bench.

"Ooo, that sounded promising."

Ruth is leaning out of her trailer door, smirking. The boys pop up behind her, grinning from ear to ear. I cover my face with both hands and groan.

"Why not?" Ruth says, stepping outside. "He's cute, single, and enjoys camping. What's not to like?"

I glance at Ethan and Gabe. "Can we talk about this later?" I mutter just loud enough for Ruth to hear. She pats me on the shoulder as the boys approach and sit down opposite me.

"Okay, so Ellie," Gabe says, "I'm a little confused. I mean, you're sorta like another grandma to me — to us — and I thought you told us that you didn't have any children. But you told Jon you've got a daughter and grandkids. So, what's up with that?"

Ethan and Gabe exchange glances. "I hope we're not out of line. If we are, just forget it," Ethan says.

"No, you're not out of line at all. It's just that I've had something extraordinary happen this summer and it has changed my whole perspective."

I tell them about my unplanned pregnancy and the shame that was piled on me for having had sex at fifteen. "Attitudes were very different back then," I explain. I describe how I bought into the shame, the humiliation. About being sent away to give birth where nobody knew me and to keep our family's "dirty laundry" a deep, dark secret. Even now, as I relate how my aunt constantly berated me for my *sinful recklessness*, I can feel my throat tighten.

"But after Lisa contacted me, I realized how ridiculous it was for me to still feel ashamed about that chapter in my life. So I had sex when I was fifteen and had a baby at sixteen. That's life. It's taken me all these years, but I have finally accepted myself and all that history. Let me tell you — it feels good to set that stigma aside."

As I talk, I watch Gabe and Ethan take each other's hand and observe how they look at one another. I'm sure they're both well acquainted with the struggle to move beyond the disapproval of others.

"Well, this has certainly been an interesting day," Ruth says, giving my arm an affectionate squeeze. "I'm going to hit the sack so I'm ready to go learn to paddleboard tomorrow."

"Rock on, Grams."

Chapter 22

Isn't it enough that I've managed to perch on my hands and knees on a paddleboard? I crawled aboard by stepping down onto it from a dock, as Gabe held tight to my hand while Ethan steadied the floating platform. I immediately crouched as low as possible to the board's surface, reluctant to even grasp the shaft of the paddle they insisted I'll need. Now, the three of them have all managed to rise to their feet on their floating crafts.

"You can do it, dear," Ruth says, maneuvering her paddleboard closer to me. "The worst thing that can happen is you'll fall into the water and have to try again."

Sucking in a deep breath, I welcome the tight fit of my life jacket. But I feel frozen in place.

"Here, take my hand," Gabe says, pulling up beside me and reaching down toward my left hand. With great trepidation, I manage to lift it to shoulder level and he grasps it. "Now, push up and place your right foot on the board."

Easier said than done. He steadies me as I move my foot and I gasp as the board wobbles. It didn't move nearly as much as I had feared, so I'm a little less nervous about following

Gabe's next instruction to get off my left knee and set that foot on the board as well. Now I'm doubled over, still bracing myself with my right hand, which is pressed against the paddle running perpendicular to the board. My butt is in the air and I'm praying that nobody takes a photo of me in this incredibly awkward pose.

"Now, stand up slowly," he says, somehow balancing on his own paddleboard while assisting me to straighten up.

They all cheer as I finally reach a standing position. "I'm letting go now," he says, opening his hand. Reluctantly, I release it and we drift apart.

I did it! I shift my weight very cautiously and adjust my feet to imitate how the others are standing. After the boys demonstrate how to manipulate my paddle, we set off on the calm, brilliant blue water, following the shoreline.

We're in a section of the lake that is somewhat separate from the main waterway, which suits me just fine. Although Gabe explained that there are "no wake" zones in the area where people are launching craft of all sizes, I prefer being in this quiet water where the only other floating object we've seen is a kayak.

After another lesson on how to propel my craft in a straight line instead of my initial circles, I begin to relax and enjoy the views. A walking path follows both shorelines, and we wave back at a father with two small children who point in our direction and jump up and down with excitement. A bit farther along, we watch a small gathering of teens leaping off a short wharf, competing for the biggest cannonball splash.

When we get close to the end of our small arm of water, we execute a broad U-turn and follow the opposite shoreline back toward our launch point.

Suddenly, I hear a rapid series of three unusually loud splashes – *bam, bam, bam*. Looking ahead, I see three people swimming to shore from beneath a high bridge. As our foursome glides slowly toward them, they emerge from the water and all dash up a steep path, apparently heading for the road that passes above the waterway across the bridge. They are youthful-looking boys – perhaps in their late teens – and all quite fit and lean.

"Did you see that?" Ethan says as we slow even further and look to see where the boys have gone.

Moments later, Gabe spots them jogging onto the bridge. "Whoa. That's what I thought," he says as the three clamber up onto the bridge's guardrail, then leap off, plunging into the lake a good fifty feet below – *bam, bam, bam.*

"Oh my God," I say, almost losing my balance after focusing on their antics. "That looks so dangerous!"

"No kidding," Ethan says. "I'm not sure they even checked that nobody was below them. Let's move over to the other shore in case they jump again."

Sure enough, in almost no time the lads reappear in the same spot and hurl themselves off, plummeting into the lake once more.

"Shouldn't we call someone?" I ask. "That can't be legal."

"Look," Ruth points out, "they're in plain sight of every car that's driven over that bridge. I'm guessing this isn't the first time those boys have pulled this stunt. What do you bet that they're on the local diving team at the high school?"

"Okay, but..."

"This is a small enough town that I'm sure lots of people know they're leaping off the bridge. I say let's leave it to the locals to decide if they want to do something about it."

"Grams, have I told you lately that you are the coolest lady on the planet?" Gabe says.

She laughs. "Not since yesterday. You always did know how to get out of a scolding by your parents for your wilder antics. Remember the time you helped Dustin climb that huge cottonwood near my home? He was what? Four years old and you were seven?"

He chuckles. "Sounds about right. Only, I don't think he had quite turned four yet. Mom was ready to tan my hide but you talked her down because I made sure I was right below him all the way up and back down again, so I could *maybe* catch him if he fell."

"I knew something your mother didn't – you had started scrambling up that same tree when *you* were four. And I followed right behind you, coaching you and hopefully keeping you as safe as possible. You were always like a little monkey, climbing everything you could. I figured nobody could stop you, so better to try to teach you how to keep from getting hurt."

"I can picture that," Ethan says. "There's no slowing down my main man, here. Sometimes he claims I've taken on the role of his mother, trying to talk some sense into him before he hurts himself."

"Does that work?" I ask.

"Never!" they declare in unison.

We float close to the dock and Gabe scampers out of the water first, then offers a hand for me to crawl out. It isn't pretty, but I manage to flop onto the platform and raise myself to a standing position without additional assistance.

"That was a blast!" Ruth says, removing her life vest.

I must admit that it really was fun, once I got the hang of it.

As we pile into their car, Gabe announces, "Okay, so we're going to stop off at the grocery store on the way back to camp. You're in for a treat, 'cause Ethan's an amazing cook and we're in charge of tonight's dinner."

Sounds good to me – I've really worked up an appetite.

***

Amazing is a great description of the meal the guys prepared. If you had asked me what Chicken Marbella was before tonight, I likely would have confused it with a number of other Italian-sounding chicken dish names, like Marsala or Piccata or Carbonara. Ethan's version included the traditional chicken, green olives, and prunes bathed in a mouth-watering marinade of vinegar, olive oil, white wine, and brown sugar. He added roasted red peppers, mushrooms, and feta cheese and served it over couscous. I ate until I thought I'd burst.

After everyone retires for the evening, I do what I've always teased others about doing – I post a photo of tonight's fare on Facebook. Gabe sent me a shot he took of Ruth and me on our paddleboards, so I share that as well and send it to Lisa with a note asking how everything is going with her and the kids. She didn't call Sunday, but I had told her we'd be on the ferry all day and wouldn't be back until late, so that's understandable. It's three hours later on the east coast than here.

I'm about to shut down my laptop when I spot an email in my spam folder from an unknown sender, **technomichael42@intellectu.al**. The topic is "hi grandma." Excited by the possibility that this is from my grandson, Michael, I open it.

> **hope it doesnt seem like i been ignorning you, real exited to meet you someday work is insane but i get time off at xmas so maybe then? if your someplace warm i could come there i like to travel haha gotta go but wanted to get in touch, more later**
>
> **M**

I've been practicing not cringing at his mother's spelling and grammar, and remind myself not to be judgmental. He's got some sort of high tech degree, so they may not have emphasized writing skills. Which reminds me that I've neglected asking for details about Michael – what he majored in, where he lives and works, what are his interests.

If he wasn't just joking about his year-end schedule, maybe the family gathering I'm hoping for will really happen! Ruth and I plan to stay in southern Arizona again this winter, so I could fly the three of them out there...

I type out a reply.

Dear Michael,

I was so pleased to hear from you! I would love to meet you in person over your Christmas break. As your mother probably told you, I live in a camper full-time, which is a significant lifestyle change for me compared to my life just a few years ago. I spend quite a bit of time hiking and enjoying the outdoors. I even went out on a stand up paddleboard (SUP) today for the first time!

This winter, I plan to be in the Phoenix area, which should be warm and sunny for your visit.

I understand you work in the high tech industry. Tell me more about your company and your position. Are you in IT or some sort of engineer?

I hope to hear from you again soon.

Love,
Grandma Ellie

Before going to bed, I jot down some ideas of places to take my family this winter in case this can all work out.

Chapter 23

"Hello, Mom? It's me." Her voice is shaky and I hear her sniff.

Is she crying? "Lisa, what's wrong?"

Her voice sounds choked. "Michael's been ... *sniff* ... in a terrible accident. Another car t-boned his and they had to rush him to the hospital."

She's definitely crying. "Is he going to be all right?" I ask, a feeling of panic causing my chest to tighten.

"He needs surgery. He has a broken pelvis and upper leg and a concussion and he's all cut up," she sobs.

This is terrible! "Are you calling from the hospital? When will he be operated on?"

"No, I'm not with him. He was travelin' for work and the accident happened in rural West Virginia, so I'm like four hours away. And he's in some Podunk little hospital in the middle of nowhere, which probably has surgeons who graduated last in their class in med school." She sniffs again, then I hear her blowing her nose. "Sorry about that. I didn't want to cry when I called you, but I can't help it."

"No, that's okay. Of course you're upset!"

"I don't want my baby havin' surgery there. What if they fu..., uh, mess it up? They're tellin' me he might never walk right again if the surgery don't go right!"

"Is he stable enough for them to transfer him to a different hospital? Maybe something closer to you?" Good heavens, there must be a number of excellent facilities in Newark and certainly just across the river in New York City!

"He's stable, alright, but his insurance won't cover the ambulance trip. I don't know what to do! I don't want my baby becomin' a cripple 'cause I couldn't get him to a good doctor." She breaks down and must be covering the phone, since the sounds grow muffled.

"Lisa?"

She clears her throat, then speaks hoarsely. "I've failed him. Lord knows I've tried, but I don't have hardly a penny left to get my baby boy to a decent hospital. I'm sorry I burdened you with this. I shouldn't of ever drug you into our lives."

"What? No, no! You are my flesh and blood, Lisa. My family. I *want* to help you and the children. Listen," I say, thinking quickly, "how much will the ambulance cost?"

"Oh no, no, no. Mom, you're not thinkin' of payin' for that, are you? No – you've already gone above and beyond for Emily."

"I insist. Now, how much for the ambulance?" Although I've always planned to leave my IRA untouched until I turn sixty-five, that's only two years away. If there ever was a good reason to withdraw some funds earlier, surely this is it.

"Four thousand dollars," she says, barely above a whisper.

Wow. Okay, that's quite a lot, but I can manage that. "I'll wire it to you right away. I agree that we want the best possible outcome for Michael, so he needs to be at a major hospital with an excellent surgical staff."

"Oh, Mom – thank you so much! This means the world to me – to us!"

"It's the least I could do. Please keep me informed all along the way on how he's doing."

"Absolutely! Well, I guess I need to get off the phone so I can arrange for the ambulance. And I need to talk to his insurance company to see what we can work out on a payment plan to cover his deductible. I know if you wait until the bill comes, they're pretty quick to start threatenin' to sic a collection agency on you, so I gotta start workin' on that right away."

I hadn't even thought of that. I've been lucky – throughout my adult life, I've always had enough put away to cover my insurance deductible, should the need arise. Not to say it wasn't a bit hit on my savings, but I had it. "How much is the deductible?" I ask.

"Oh," she sighs. "Let me think. All this bad news has my brain all messed up, you know?" She pauses. "Okay, yeah. It's two thousand dollars."

"Consider it covered. You have more important things to focus on than medical bills. Go make that call and go be with your son when he's transferred. That's what's important right now."

"Oh, Mom. You are a life saver! I don't know how we can ever thank you enough."

"You just did. Now go – get Michael moved to a good hospital and call me once he's there, okay?"

"Absolutely. We love you, Mom."

I have to gasp for air, the words squeezing my heart. "I love all of you, too. Talk to you later."

Oh, my. I'm so worried for Michael, but so moved by Lisa's words that I can hardly think straight. But I've got to get my act together and take care of the money transfers.

Logging on to the website for the financial services company that manages my IRA, it takes me several minutes to figure out how to withdraw funds from my account. I'm old enough that there isn't a penalty for taking the money out, but I will have to pay taxes on it as if I earned the additional $6,000 as income. Again, that's something I can manage.

Unfortunately, if I want to wire the money to a bank account that I haven't already set up on their website, there will be a delay of up to a week. That won't do. Instead, I transfer the funds directly to my personal bank account, hoping I'll be able to turn right around and wire money from there to Lisa's bank.

I'm able to order the wire transfer, but see that the funds won't go out until tomorrow morning, since the original IRA transfer has to clear first. Hoping that delay won't be a problem, I call her back to let her know. The call goes to voicemail.

"Lisa, I wanted to let you know that the funds won't get to you until tomorrow. I hope that doesn't create a problem! Maybe the ambulance company doesn't need the money up front? Or you can show them that the wire transfer is pending. Let me know what they say, and I'm really sorry the money won't be there for you today." I tap my fingers on the table in frustration. "Love you," I say, hanging up.

I need to move around, I'm so worked up. Shoving my phone in my pocket, I head outside and stride anxiously through the campground, imagining the young man in the photos Lisa sent now lying in a hospital emergency room, hooked up to machines, doctors and nurses hovering over him. I picture him being wheeled into surgery – but is it in a large, modern hospital or a small, out-of-date one?

"Hey, Grams. I mean – sorta Grams."

It's Gabe. He chuckles at his slip. I stop my quick march and stop my racing thoughts and offer up a pathetic attempt at a laugh. "Hi. Sorry, my mind was elsewhere."

"No problem. So, what do you think if Ethan and I call you Grandma Sorta?"

"Grandma what?"

"Sorta. Since you're sorta like another grandma to us."

Grandma Sorta. It's odd, but also touching that the boys consider me to be almost family. Who'd have thought I'd be gaining all these family members at this stage of my life!

"I like it," I tell him.

"So, we're thinking of driving up into the mountains and hiking around a small lake I found on the map. You wanna go?"

"Normally I would, but I'm waiting for an important call," I say, pulling my phone out of my pocket as if that might magically cause it to ring. There might not be coverage if we drive up into the hills. I glance at the screen and realize that there's a text message waiting for me – from Lisa! I was so wrapped up in my thoughts that I never heard the notification.

"Hold on a second," I tell Gabe as I access the message.

no problem i got 10 days to pay them :)
thanks again!!! xxxooo

I let out a long breath. "Looks like I can join you after all."

Chapter 24

As Ethan drives all of us to the lake, I explain what's going on with my grandson.

"That's frightening news, dear, but thank goodness he's being moved to a major medical center," Ruth says, grasping my hand. Gabe twists around in the passenger seat and reaches back toward me. I squeeze his hand with my free one.

"I hope they've got him on plenty of pain meds for that long ride in the ambulance," he says.

"I'm sure they will," Ruth says. "Hopefully, he'll be so out of it that he won't even remember the trip once all this is over."

Ethan catches my eye in his rear-view mirror. "He must have a great insurance policy. There was this woman I know from work who had to be transferred to a Level 1 Trauma Center after being in a nasty car wreck a couple of years ago. She and her husband had a ton of hassles proving to the insurance company that the ambulance was necessary so they'd cover it."

"Actually, his insurance isn't going to pay for it." I hesitate to tell them where the money is coming from – I don't want it to sound like I'm tooting my own horn.

"But you said they're tight on funds. How are they going to manage?" Ruth asks, a worried frown on her face.

I pause, unwilling to lie but searching for a way to answer without really answering. Gabe jumps in before I have to end the gap in the conversation. "They could set up one of those online funding things. I'll bet they've got friends who would pitch in and post about it on social media. We could even help spread the word. Don't you think that would work, Ethan?"

"Sure. It's worth a shot," he answers. "If they need help setting it up, I'd be glad to help out, Grandma Sorta." His New England accent has it sounding like *Gramasoda*.

It's great to have an IT expert in the family. However, now I really need to set the record straight so Ethan doesn't post something misleading online asking for funds they already have.

"Actually, that may not be necessary," I say, biting my lower lip. "I've taken care of the ambulance cost."

"Oh?" Ethan looks back at me with raised eyebrows.

"Although it's possible there'll be additional expenses in the future. You know, co-pays or items not fully covered. And I have no idea what his work situation will be if he's out for an extended period of time, which I'm sure he will be. So thanks for the offer, Ethan. I may need your help with something like that down the road."

We've arrived at the lake, so Ethan parks and we all emerge from the car and fetch our packs.

Ruth speaks to me quietly as the boys go to read the information signs on the kiosk by the trailhead. "Ellie, dear, if you don't mind my asking, how much did that set you back?"

I tell her and her eyes grow wide, but she doesn't comment further. We catch up with Gabe and Ethan and set out on our hike around the pretty little lake, the surrounding mountains reflecting in its still waters.

After a few minutes, Ethan slows down to walk beside me.

"Tell me again how you and your daughter found each other," he says, so I tell him about her Facebook messages and how she had been contacting every person she could find whose name matched mine.

"Lucky thing I included Driskel, my maiden name, on my Facebook page," I say. "She had no way of knowing my married name was Dwyer."

"Yeah," he says, and we hike for a few minutes longer. Up ahead of us, Ruth and Gabe are laughing and picking up their pace.

"So," he says, "how did she know to search for the name Eleanor Driskel? You said the adoption records were secret."

"I wondered that myself. Lisa explained that the records become available to the child and the birth parents if the adoptive parents are deceased and the child is at least 21."

"Huh. I never knew that. But then again, the people I know who were adopted have always had some contact with their birth parents. I guess things were different back then."

"Most definitely," I say, pausing for a moment to retrieve a bottle from an outside pocket of my pack and gulp down some water. "When I was in my teens, I don't think I'd ever heard of an adoption where any contact information was available for either the birth parents or the adoptive family. Now, though, I think that sort of secrecy is fairly rare."

It's hard to imagine how different my life and Lisa's would have been if we had been able to contact each other or even meet regularly throughout her life. Obviously, I would have had to share my history with Franklin. If this had all happened years later, when the stigma of having a baby outside of marriage had faded to almost nothing, then perhaps my parents wouldn't have felt so ashamed of me and they wouldn't have sent me away to have the baby in secret. I wouldn't have spent the summer with Aunt Phyllis and endured three months of constant criticism and shaming – daily reminders of my *immorality* and other name-calling, using terms I still find shocking today.

If only we had been able to find each other sooner, I might have been able to help her get the education she hoped for.

We catch up with Gabe and his grandmother, who have taken a break to sit and gaze at the gorgeous scenery. I've been so wrapped up in my thoughts that I've barely noted the fluffy clouds and soaring peaks above the turquoise waters. It's marvelous.

During the drive back to camp, Gabe and Ruth are relating entertaining stories from his childhood. Like the time he jumped off the roof of the garage while holding a bed sheet, thinking it would act as a parachute.

"I wasn't entirely stupid. I did blow up an air mattress and aim for that. I didn't break anything. But I sprained my ankle pretty badly."

Ruth shakes her head. "And destroyed the air mattress, of course." They both burst out laughing. "Did I ever tell you that your mother tried something similar when she was about the same age?"

"No way!"

"Yep. Only she jumped out of a tree into one of those above ground pools that's about three feet deep. Broke her big toe."

"Wow – she never told me about that!" Again, they find this hilarious.

Oh my God – this family! They're crazy, but I love them. "Ruth, you realize these stories aren't helping to convince me to join you on future adventures."

The tales continue and I realize that Ethan has been unusually quiet. I can see his upper face in the rear-view mirror, and he seems deep in thought. Surely he's heard some of these stories before or at least knows that his partner is hardly a quiet, cautious human being.

***

The next morning, as I prepare a fruit salad to go with our breakfast, I'm surprised when I glance out my window and spot Ethan walking toward my campsite. Has there been a change in plans? I open my door and call out, "Good morning, Ethan. Isn't this a pretty day!"

"Hi, Grandma Sorta." *Gramasoda! So cute.* "I wanted to check something out with you. Would you mind showing me the original message you got from your daughter?"

"Oh, well – sure. Here you go," I say, opening my Facebook app on my phone and locating our online conversation. As I hand it to him, I ask, "Is something wrong?" He looks so serious.

"Give me a sec," he says, his thumbs moving quickly to scroll through the page, then tap on this and that. I've never managed to learn to type on my phone with my thumbs – I tap out text with painfully slow pokes at my screen with one forefinger.

"Hmm," he says.

"What?"

"Another sec."

Finally, he looks up at me and chews on his lower lip. "There might be a problem."

"What kind of problem?" I say, starting to feel nervous.

"So, I was looking at Lisa's Facebook page, and see that she just set it up about a week before she contacted you."

"Well, she said she doesn't have a lot of time to use Facebook and all that."

"See how she only has three Facebook 'Friends' besides you? Now, look at this." He taps and scrolls, then holds the phone so I can see it.

"Wait," I say. "That's Lisa's photo but the name says Abigail Hindlestor. Why is this Abigail person using Lisa's photo?"

The expression on his face is one of pity. "I think it's the other way around. Look," he says, placing a hand on my shoulder, "Last night, I did a little research on closed adoptions. That whole thing about the records being available if the adoptive parents die? I couldn't find anything to confirm that. However, I did find an old article about some rural county records in the Midwest getting hacked several years ago. It was thought that the hackers were able to obtain adoption data along with a variety of other information."

It's starting to sink in. "Are you saying that Lisa might be an imposter? Does that mean that this Abigail is really my daughter?" Have I sent all that money to the wrong person?

He sighs. "No, I just think *Lisa*," he draws air quotes when he says her name, "stole Abigail's profile photo and used it to set up a fake account. Where do you have the photos she sent of herself and her children?"

He hands me back my phone but my hand is trembling so badly I have trouble calling up the pictures.

"Here, let me help," he says. "Ah, here they are." I sit down and bury my face in my hands. After a minute or so, he comes over to me to show me what I now expect to be more bad news.

I'm right.

Ethan has found a picture of a little girl I thought was Emily in a kitty costume identical to the photo Lisa sent me. It appears in a blog called Connie's Comments. The caption reads, "Zoey is ready for trick-or-treating, teeth or no teeth!" Ethan scrolls through the blog and little Zoey appears in numerous other places. He switches to another website and there is a serious young teenager wearing a blue tie and dark jacket, standing between a man and woman. The shot is the one I received where people were obviously cropped out of the photo. "Jacob and his proud parents at his bar mitzvah," the caption reads. The article is dated from earlier this year.

"Oh my God," I moan. "None of them are really who I thought?"

"No, I don't think so. I'm so sorry to bring you such bad news, Grandma Sorta. I know you were really excited to hook up with your daughter. You said you'd already taken care of what you thought were the ambulance costs. I think you need to get on the phone with your bank or credit card company right away and tell them to put a stop payment on that money. Tell them what happened. They should know what to do next to try to catch this scam artist."

I'm such an idiot. How could I have made such a big mistake? While Ethan goes to tell the others that breakfast will be delayed, I wrangle my way through phone menu options for my bank, getting put on hold after I'm told I've reached the wrong department. I dab at my eyes with a tissue and take a quick sip of water, trying desperately to hold it together and not start crying on the phone.

I'm far more upset about losing what I thought was my family than about the money. Over this past couple of months, I fell in love with the people who now turn out to be total fabrications. I can't believe I fell for this scam! I'm an intelligent, educated person. How could I have been so stupid?

"Hello, Ms. Dwyer? This is Lisa in Security and Fraud Prevention. How may I help you?"

Seriously – *her* name is Lisa, too? Heaven help me.

Thankfully, Security Lisa doesn't treat me like I'm an imbecile. She's calm, understanding ("This happens far more often than you might think"), and professional. She also breaks the news that the $2,000 I sent for "Emily's" college fees and course supplies cannot be retrieved. "Not unless we're able to track down the people running this scam," she explains. "However, let me see if the $6,000 wire for today has been processed yet."

She puts me on hold and I listen to the same, annoying music loop at least fifty times before she comes back on the line.

"Ms. Dwyer – are you still on the line?"

"Yes, I'm here." Please tell me I didn't call too late to stop the transfer.

"I'm sorry," she says, and I barely register the rest of the sentence. What a fool I was! That horrible con artist stole $8,000 from me. If not for Ethan, how much more might I have thrown away?

I tune back into Security Lisa's voice as she explains that wiring money the way I did is one of the least safe ways to transfer money to someone I don't know. And here I thought it was a smart way to go. By the time we get off the phone, she's helped me get the legal wheels rolling on attempting to identify who Phony Lisa really is. Security Lisa tells me not to get my hopes up. "Scammers like this are very hard to track down. Even if they are apprehended, the money may never be recovered." I'm advised to sit tight and not respond if she contacts me again, but to pass along any messages I might receive.

When I end the call, I burst into tears. For all these years, I've managed to bury my memories of my child's birth and any curiosity about what became of her. Now this cruel, greedy person has brought it all to the forefront of my mind and caused me to actually *long* to connect with my daughter. And I never will. The records are sealed.

Clutching a pillow to my chest, I sob, feeling as if my child and grandchildren have all been ripped from my heart. It's as if I've learned that my entire family has died far, far away from me and I don't even know their names.

"Ellie?" I hear Ruth tap on the door, but I'm not ready to be with anyone.

"I can't talk to you right now," I call out. "Please leave me alone."

I shove my pillow over my face so she won't hear me crying. She doesn't knock again, so I think she's left.

Chapter 25

It's quite early, but Gabe and Ethan are already packing up to head back home so they can return to work tomorrow morning. I barely slept last night, but didn't want to miss saying goodbye to my *sorta* grandsons. They may be as close as I'll ever get now to having an extended family. Reminding myself of my resolution to focus on the positive in light of sorrowful times, I strive to put on a happy demeanor and focus on the warm relationship I've developed with these young men.

"Thanks for a great time, Grams and Grandma Sorta," Gabe says, hugging each of us tightly.

Ethan follows suit. "We'll miss you two." To me, he adds, "Let me know how things go with the investigation. I hope they catch those scumbags, but I wouldn't hold my breath. You take care of yourself, okay?"

I nod and hug him again. "Thanks for saving my hide. God knows how much longer I would have been sucked into that woman's scheme and how much more money I would have sent her."

"Or them. It could be an entire team of scammers."

I hadn't even thought of that. Despite knowing that the photos and names were all fake, I still imagine a pretty, brown-haired, 47-year-old American woman behind all this mess. It could just as well be a gang of geeky, twenty-year-old hackers from Russia.

As the boys drive off, Ruth and I wave until they're out of sight. She turns to me and declares, "All right, then. You and I need to sit down and write up a plan for having as much fun as possible during our last week here. I'll grab some notes I jotted down already, and I'll meet you at your place so we can research ideas on your laptop."

"Right now?"

She's already marching toward her camper. "Do you have anything better to do right now?" she calls back over her shoulder. The unspoken message is, "Let's get your mind off the whole adoption fiasco." Good idea.

We spend nearly an hour scanning maps and reading trip reports and reviews, and come up with a list of activities and destinations in the area that could fill two weeks. "I need a few days this week to work," I say, my mind veering back to my recent financial blunders. All that money is long gone, unless they track down the scammers.

"Two full days, or what?"

My work requires a very high level of concentration, and I tend to get bleary-eyed if I try to focus for more than an hour at a time. Realistically, I can only manage around three to four one-hour blocks in a day. "Let's call it two half days."

"Perfect." She scans our list, drawing a large star beside two entries. "A half day of work and a half day of play. Now, if we can get going in the next thirty minutes, we have enough time for almost any of these other items. Which shall we do today?"

"Were you a drill sergeant in a former life?" I ask, shaking my head but grinning. Truth is, I'm extremely thankful to have such an enthusiastic friend. Finding interesting things to do to keep my mind off the Lisa affair is just what I need.

***

Am I really doing this? I smile nervously as I approach Jon's motorhome, carrying a box containing two slices of double-chocolate cake from the supermarket bakery as my contribution to tonight's dinner.

Ruth has been on my case for the past several days, urging me to take Jon up on his invitation to have dinner with him. "You'll probably have fun," she insists. Well, it *is* another way to focus on something other than my recent woes. So, here I am.

I keep telling myself, "This is not a date, just dinner with a new friend," but I can't quite convince myself. After all, he clearly invited *only* me. It's a date.

"Hello, hello!" he says, hurrying down the stairs from his rig. "Welcome, Ellie."

"Hi." I can't think of anything else to say. I take in the delicious aroma of something sizzling on the shiny barbeque grill sitting beside his picnic table. There is absolutely no place in my little camper where I could store something that large, but with his impressive motorhome, there are storage compartments nearly the size of my entire kitchen and dining table. "Smells wonderful," I say, setting down the dessert on the table.

"Hope you like lamb chops," he says, then steps closer to the cake and takes a peep at it. "Wow – how did you know I'm a chocaholic?"

"It takes one to know one," I reply, thankful that my tongue has seemingly come untied. "And yes, I love lamb chops, although I haven't eaten any for ages." Franklin used to crave them, and we'd grill some several times during the summers. Naturally, I don't share that memory with Jon.

We lounge in a pair of comfy outdoor chairs as the meal

cooks, sharing glasses of red wine and stories of our camping adventures. And mishaps.

"I was camped for several days in northwestern Texas when we got word of a tornado warning in the area," he says. "Talk about scared! Everyone in camp fled to the concrete restrooms and packed ourselves inside to wait it out. Fortunately, some had the foresight to bring blankets or cushions to sit on, and flashlights."

"Eww. Not my idea of a good time. Did it stink?"

He crinkles his nose. "Not as bad as it could have been, but it wasn't good. After almost four hours of taking turns sitting on the closed commode or on the floor, we got the all clear from the campground manager. Nothing touched down close enough to do any serious damage, but there were plenty of new 'lakes' all around camp and lots of small stuff scattered about."

"I'm not sure how my lightweight camper would do in a situation like that. I've had it parked in some pretty windy conditions, but nothing approaching a tornado!"

We both turn to look at his touring-bus sized motorhome. "Judging from pictures I've seen, even this 20,000 pound baby can be tossed around like a matchstick if a twister gets hold of it."

I tell him about the time my refrigerator door popped open while I was driving to a new campsite. "Not only did I end up with fresh veggies scattered across the floor, there was a container of this nut and cranberry gelatin salad I made. It had popped open and spilled everywhere. You know what happens when Jello gets warm?"

"Hmm. I imagine it gets rather gooey and sticky." He winces.

"You imagine right. That took me hours to clean up. And the worst thing?"

He raises his eyebrows. "Tell me."

"I've installed a strap to lock the refrigerator door closed when I travel. I just forgot to fasten it that time." I shake my head and chuckle.

The meal is delicious and I'm amazed when I realize that we've been visiting for almost three hours. This has been a fun evening after all. Jon is a good cook, funny, listens closely to what I say, and – best of all – hasn't brought up the subject of children or grandchildren. The last thing I wanted to do tonight is explain that I was mistaken when I told him about my family.

As the late September twilight fades, I help him carry our dirty dishes inside, then reach for the kitchen sink faucet to start rinsing them. "Oh, no Ellie. Just leave them. I'll take care of the dishes."

He gives me the grand tour of his unit, and it truly is grand! The story of Goldilocks pops into my head. Some people would say my teeny A-frame camper is too small, Jon's mansion of a unit is too big, and Ruth's modest-sized trailer is just right. While this place feels roomy and luxurious to me, I shudder at the thought of learning to drive it around and park it! My cozy trailer suits me just fine.

Sensing that I'm ready to depart, Jon insists on just one more story. He points to a gap beneath the sofa. "I was having problems with the slides for a storage drawer under here, so I removed the drawer entirely. Anyway, I had been careless with keeping my door shut and when I came inside one night, I could hear something moving around under there."

"A mouse?" I ask.

He shakes his head. "Definitely bigger. I shined a flashlight and two eyes were glowing back at me. I figured it was somebody's cat that got in. I was reluctant to reach for it, in case it was feral. So I placed a small bowl of water in front of the couch, hoping it would come out to investigate. After waiting a few hours, it appeared that the kitty wasn't tempted enough by water to come out, so I tried milk instead. Still nothing."

"How long had it been there by that point?"

He shrugs. "Maybe three hours. It was getting pretty late and I really wanted to head to bed, so I decided to take my chances. I propped the outside door open just enough for the cat to squeeze through and went to bed, figuring the odds were good that nobody was going to sneak in and steal something during the night."

"Was it gone in the morning?" I ask, becoming more intrigued by his story.

"No. This time I offered it some cut-up steak I had left over from earlier in the week. Tried coaxing it out by calling, 'Here kitty, kitty, kitty' while crouched on the floor. Then I backed off and watched for it to emerge, but eventually gave up and left to go for a hike or something. When I got back, the dish was clean and the glowing eyes were still back there. Well, this went on for another two days. I kept placing the food farther and farther from the sofa, and calling, "Here kitty, kitty," but that darn cat always waited until I was gone to eat it."

"They're clever little creatures, aren't they?"

He nods. "Definitely. So I realized I'd have to only leave food while I was here. I picked out a good book to read, sat right over there where I'd be out of its line of sight but close to the dish, and waited it out."

"And?"

"After an hour or so, here comes my little buddy. Mostly black with beautiful long fur and a bushy tail. And a white stripe along its back."

My mouth drops open with the image. "A skunk?"

"Pepé Le Pew, or one of his friends. Thankfully, he seemed to appreciate that I was friend, not foe. I eased my way to the refrigerator, retrieved the rest of the chopped up meat, and headed out the front door, leaving a track of goodies leading outside. It took a bit of coaching. Calling out, "Here, skunky, skunky," may or may not have helped, but Pepé eventually waddled his way out of here without leaving a calling card."

We've stepped outside as he spoke, following the path his little visitor may have taken. Jon walks me back to my campsite, a journey of about a hundred yards. This was fun, but now I'm fretting about the protocol of ending the evening. I hope he doesn't want to kiss me. I haven't been on a "date" for over forty years or kissed anyone besides Franklin. I am so not ready for a kiss.

"Goodnight, Ellie. This was fun," he says, leaning toward me. Frozen in place, I'm relieved when he pecks me on the cheek.

I smile broadly. "I had a fun time, too. Thanks for dinner and all the great stories."

"Let's keep in touch," he says. "I hope we can do this again."

"I do too."

With that, our date is over. Ruth and I are starting our way south in just a few days, so Jon and I are unlikely to spend another evening together like this before we depart. We've shared contact information and he says he plans to spend part of the winter in southern Arizona as are Ruth and I, so perhaps we *will* see each other again.

See, Ellie, I tell myself. There's life after Franklin after all.

***

My fake daughter hasn't been in touch since I wired the money for "Michael." Maxwell, my key contact with the fraud investigation, informs me that Phony Lisa closed the bank account that received my funds immediately after the $6,000 was deposited. He's had me send more and more desperate-sounding messages asking about the health of my grandson, but now that a week has gone by, it's clear that she's long gone.

"Do you think you'll find whoever this is? Can you trace her when she uses her cell phone, or how does that work?" I ask him.

"Sorry, Mrs. Dwyer, but we can't share those sort of details of the investigation. If we do apprehend the person or persons who contacted you, we'll let you know. We appreciate your cooperation."

Reading between the lines, it seems unlikely that they'll ever catch up with "Lisa" now that she's got the money. Ethan has explained to me how easy it is to set up a fake Facebook account, a bogus email address, and to use a throwaway cell phone. I wonder if she's set up other false identities. How many people has she stolen from? I may never know.

Chapter 26

As the warm days fade into chilly nights, we begin our journey southward, eventually to wind up just outside Phoenix, which we plan to use as a home base for the winter. Splitting up our long trip, we're spending a week near Twin Falls, Idaho and our bodies begin adjusting to the cooler autumn temperatures. Most of our hikes are centered around viewing fabulous waterfalls and the dramatic canyon formed by the Snake River. We've just returned to the start of a stunning walk along the canyon rim when Ruth points to a group of people on the high suspension bridge over the river, which has been the object of many of my photos during our stay.

"Look," she says, pulling a small pair of binoculars from her pack and raising them to her face. "I think they're getting ready to jump off!"

We've seen brochures describing BASE jumping, which is apparently quite popular in this area. I've heard of other locations where people choose to leap off things that are described by the BASE acronym: Buildings, Antennae, Spans (such as a bridge), and high cliffs (the "E" stands for Earth) and float to the ground using a rectangular-shaped parachute.

All the stories I've read seemed to be about people jumping where it wasn't legal. Here, the sport is clearly embraced by the local tourism industry.

"Someone's climbing up on the railing," Ruth says. "It's a woman!"

I use my phone camera's zoom to try to get a better look before deciding I prefer not seeing her face before she possibly falls to her death. My palms have gone clammy.

We both gasp as she vaults off the bridge, her arms and legs extended in a giant X.

"Oh my God," I whisper. "Her parachute isn't opening!" I press my hands over my mouth and order myself not to look, but I can't seem to turn away.

Boom! Her parachute snaps open with a sound that reverberates like a gunshot and echoes in the canyon. A rainbow-striped canopy arcs above her as she soars in lazy s-curves to the riverbank far below us.

"Ellie, I wonder if they offer tandem rides," Ruth says, grinning like a kid in a candy store.

"No, no, no," I say, shaking my head vehemently. "I am *not* going to try that. No. Absolutely not. And I'm not going to come watch if you do it. I almost had a heart attack watching a total stranger."

"Where's your sense of adventure, dear?"

"I don't equate adventure with insanity, that's all."

It doesn't surprise me in the least when she calls around to see if she can participate in falling off a great height while strapped to someone she's known for about fifteen minutes, then rely on that stranger to save her from plummeting to her death. Of course, that's not how she words it.

Much to my relief, there are no open booking slots available in the next two days before we plan to move on to warmer climes.

"I'll plan ahead better next time," she says.

Oh, Ruth. How did you ever manage to survive to be eighty-two?

***

We're headed in different directions for this coming week. I'm driving to Las Vegas, where I'll meet up with my old friends and neighbors, Claire and Otis Williamson. Back when Franklin and I had our California home in the hills, we got together with them regularly for game nights or movie nights. Claire and I – along with our neighbor Nan, with whom we've both lost touch – used to roam around the winding roads in our area, lusting over the upscale homes and landscaping on the hillsides above our neighborhood. Sadly, the wildfires that raged through those valleys devastated many of those properties. Our home survived, untouched by flames, but smoke, water, and chemical retardant left us with a choice of making substantial repairs or moving. We chose to move. Claire and Otis stayed and rebuilt.

Who made the better choice? Well, so far their area has avoided additional wildfires. Our next home on the east coast was in the path of a major hurricane. So there you have it.

I'm excited but a little anxious about this upcoming get-together with my friends. I'm also proud of myself for initiating contact with them after a gap of several years. At least I can get *this* reunion to happen. I'm sure I'll never connect with my real daughter. Thank goodness the Williamsons are childless – we won't have to catch up on news of children and grandchildren. I don't think I could handle that at this point. Also, during our phone conversations over the past year or so, we've come to an implicit understanding to only mention Franklin during the "good" times we all shared – no rehashing of the turmoil after he pulled his *Disappearing Act*.

"Ellie – is that you?" Claire shouts, scurrying across the

170

hotel lobby to great me with a hug. "You look fantastic! So skinny! And I love your hair that color."

Skinny? That's a huge exaggeration. Still, I have dropped some weight since we last saw each other. As for my hair, I've stopped coloring it, so this is my natural gray.

"You look great too," I say, hugging her back. The truth is, the California sun has not been kind to her skin – she looks considerably older than I remember. Still, it's wonderful to see her again.

"Hi, Ellie." Otis gives me a brief hug. He and Franklin were close, but I never felt like I knew Otis all that well. When we'd all get together, the men would often end up talking in one room while the women gathered in another.

"Let's get you checked in and then how about the lunch buffet?" Claire says.

This will be quite a change to my routine. Claire found an incredibly inexpensive hotel package for our two rooms at this hotel with a casino, so I'll be sleeping in a room larger than my entire "house" for the next two nights. My camper is folded down and parked in a huge, gated lot nearby, still hooked up to my Jeep. I feel like a traitor, abandoning it!

At the buffet, I try not to load up my plate too badly, figuring I won't be getting much exercise these next few days, although I'm hoping I can convince Claire to drive us to some interesting-looking neighborhoods so we can walk around like we used to, gawking at the properties just for fun. Otis, who has grown remarkably larger since I saw him last, doesn't hold back as he helps himself to a boatload of crab legs, a mountain of mashed potatoes, and a generous selection of every fried food known to mankind. Claire shows far more restraint and I catch her rolling her eyes when he sets his first helping on our table.

Picturing the scene in *Close Encounters of the Third Kind* where Richard Dreyfus sculpts his mashed potatoes into a model of Devil's Tower, I try not to stare as Otis consumes his food.

"Our life is so predictable," Claire says when I ask for an update. "I spend a lot of time at the pool – a little bit of swimming but more often reading – and Otis tinkers with his model trains. You should see the little villages and miniature cliffs topped by trees that he's built! We were so upset when his original models were damaged, but he's rebuilt and expanded far beyond what he had before." Otis pulls out his phone and shows me several shots of his creative and impressive hobby.

"Tell us about all *your* adventures," Claire says, so I launch into stories about how Ruth and I decided to travel together, especially focusing on our recent visit to the Pacific Northwest, seasoning my tales with corresponding photos on my phone.

"Here's a shot of the lake we started from that morning," I say, showing them the oblong turquoise waters in a valley at least a thousand feet below where I was hiking. "And here we've hiked down to the next valley and we're waiting for a boat to take us back around to the trailhead, instead of hiking all that way over the pass again."

"Goodness," Claire says. "I can't imagine walking all that way. Ellie, you've become quite the athlete! What's your secret, taking up hiking at our age?"

Ha! At *our* age? The photos I've shown of Ruth have all been at a distance and she's had on a hat to hide her spiky, white hair. "Claire, as I recall, you're two years younger than I am – sixty-one, right?" She nods.

"Well, my friend Ruth here is eighty-two. I guess I'd have to say that *she* is my secret. When we first met, I could hardly hike a mile if there was any sort of hill, and I didn't believe I could get fit because I was about to turn sixty. But after being around her, I suppose I've become infected by her enthusiasm and energy. We have a blast!"

"Well, I find that inspiring, Ellie. Maybe I can catch some

of that energy from you and start thinking differently about what I do. Tell you what," she says, dabbing her lips with her napkin and pushing her plate away, "what if I start today? How about we drive around and find a ritzy neighborhood and go explore it on foot, like we used to do?"

Otis goes wide-eyed and shakes his head very subtly, probably hoping I don't notice. "Dear, would you like to join us, or would you rather check out the casino this afternoon?" his wife asks, diplomatically giving him the opportunity to do his own thing.

"Yeah, I think I'd like to try my hand at blackjack," he says.

"Good. That'll give us girls a chance to really catch up. Do you mind if we excuse ourselves so we can get going?"

"No problem," Otis says. "I'll see you ladies later, then."

And we're off.

Chapter 27

Two days of casinos and crowds were quite enough for me, thank you very much. I must admit that I thoroughly enjoyed attending the Blue Man Group show last night, and spending time with my friends helped keep my mind off my recent fiasco, but still it's good to be setting up camp again. Ruth arrives tomorrow night, after a short visit to Moab, Utah where she stopped briefly at Arches and Canyonlands National Parks.

"We've got to come back to this area next spring," she tells me over the phone. "We could easily spend a month exploring the two national parks here."

Growing up in the Denver area, I remember a trip with my parents to Arches one summer. It was exceptionally hot, so we pretty much stayed in the car and drove from viewpoint to viewpoint. Now that I'm a bona fide hiker, I'd love to return in a milder season and explore the amazing rock formations up close. "I'm sold," I tell her. "I'll research the monthly temperatures and we'll pick the dates."

Today I'll catch up on work, then review maps of the area and start picking out some hikes and places to visit. Get the lay of the land, as it were. We won't move into our long-term campground for another two weeks. Meanwhile, we've chosen a state park east of the Phoenix metropolitan area so we can check out destinations in the Superstition Mountains.

Number one on my list is Boyce Thompson Arboretum, about a half hour drive from here. Very shortly after I started camping, I met a delightful couple – the Russells – who had been traveling around the western U.S. for several years. They highly recommended this destination, along with many others, and I scanned their hand-written pages of ideas onto my phone. I've visited several of their suggestions, and all have been spot on.

Speaking of the Russells, I haven't been in touch with them for ages. Here's another opportunity for me to break out of my shell and reach out to people who have been kind and helpful to me. As I recall, Bernie and Annie contacted *me* last. I dawdled and procrastinated so long in replying that I eventually convinced myself that it would seem weird for me to finally answer.

That's exactly the sort of habit I'm trying to break. I fire off an email to them, letting them know my current plans and asking where their travels have taken them. They'll be so pleased to learn how well I've adjusted to camping life – I was such a newbie when I met them! Maybe I can even offer *them* some suggestions about places to visit, now that I've become a seasoned traveler.

Feeling pleased with myself, I hunker down to finish up my latest project so I'll be free to get out and play when Ruth arrives.

Three hours later, I decide my eyes have had enough for now. Time for a break. I log into Facebook and scan through the updates from my online friends and interests, but then my curiosity gets the better of me, and call up my message history, curious if "Lisa" has ever posted there again.

When I click on our online conversation, it looks quite different than before. Where it once showed *Lisa Johnson* and displayed her profile picture beside her comments, now there's just a gray circle and the generic name, *Facebook User*. I try to pull up her page but it no longer exists. There are plenty of other *Lisa Johnsons* to be found on Facebook, but not the one who claimed to be my daughter. Whether this means the authorities have caught up with her, or if she's the one who deleted her account, I don't know. I assume it's the latter.

I sink back in my seat and a feeling of loss envelops me – again. Some part of me still hoped this was all just a misunderstanding – my daughter wasn't really a lying scam artist. Maybe some *other* Lisa Johnson would step forward and claim me as her mother.

"Damn her." I had spent a lifetime burying the whole teenage pregnancy memory and was perfectly content pretending to myself and everyone around me that I had never given birth. Now look at me! I find myself wondering about my *real* daughter, longing to connect with my child. How do I erase these feelings and go back to where I once was?

Maybe once Ruth arrives, I'll feel better. She always seems so insightful about life's challenges, and immersing myself in our joint adventures will certainly do me good.

***

My camping friends were absolutely correct – the arboretum is well worth a long visit. They could have called it a lush desert botanical garden, with its acres of remarkable displays of dry climate vegetation from around the world. Ruth and I wander its many curving paths to discover oases of blooming cactus, palms, herbs, and flowers. As the day heats up, we roam through a Eucalyptus grove and follow a trail beneath rugged cliffs.

"Look at that!" Ruth exclaims, pointing up into the crotch of an enormous tree ahead. "What is it?"

With its long, narrow snout and a ring of white fur around

its eyes, my first thought is some sort of light-colored raccoon. It changes position, and we spot its incredibly long, furry, striped tail.

"I have no idea what it is," I say, "but it's beautiful." I manage to snap a few photos before the creature swiftly climbs down the tree head-first, and scampers off into the woods, its magnificent tail held high like a cat's, but much longer.

After exploring as many side trails as we can, we find a bench to sit and rest our weary feet before making our way back to the gift shop. We only get lost twice trying to find the way.

I show off my photos of the unusual animal to the employee behind the counter. "That's a coatimundi," she says, "or coati for short. It's native to this area, and on down into South America."

"Are they dangerous?" I ask.

She laughs. "I wouldn't call them dangerous. Actually, I know someone who raised one as a pet, although I don't think that's a good idea – they aren't a domestic animal, and they have sharp teeth and claws. But if we just give them a little space to roam around and climb trees and root for food, then everybody's happy."

I buy a colorful lizard sculpture as a thank you gift for Ethan and Gabe for saving me from turning my big mistake into an even greater financial disaster. I'm lucky to have a computer geek in my "family."

***

Days later, when the boys call to thank me for the artwork, we chat for several minutes about what we two Grandmas have been up to since they departed. They've clearly got their phone on speaker, since both comment when I describe the unusual animal we encountered. "I totally want to find a pet store and get us a coati," Gabe announces.

"Last month you said you wanted an ocelot, man. And before that it was a boa constrictor. I keep telling you, let's just get a small dog or a really cool *domestic* cat like Charli," Ethan says.

"Anybody can have a cat or dog."

"Exactly." Ethan clears his throat and his tone turns serious. "So – whole different topic. Here's the thing. I've been doing some research." He hesitates.

"About...?" I prompt.

"About adoptees and adoptive parents reconnecting."

Oh, dear. That's what I was afraid of. Part of me deeply regrets exhuming that chapter from my distant past. Rebury the memories, forget about my daughter who is an absolute stranger to me, and reclaim my life. But another little voice keeps piping up, asking questions about that stranger's life, about how she felt about me while growing up, and how she feels now. Has she led a happy life? Does she look like me, share any of my traits?

"Okay," I say, keeping my tone noncommittal. "And what did you learn?" *Why am I doing this to myself?*

He tells me about several online websites, including one in the state of Iowa, where I gave birth. "These are totally legit," he tells me. It seems that I can register on one or more of them, providing the date and location of my child's birth. If she also searches those databases, she has the option of asking to share contact information with me. It almost sounds like a dating site.

"You're saying we both have to agree to the contact?" I ask.

"Exactly. So, it's a crap shoot. You could register on all these sites and do a search for her, but if she hasn't ever registered, nothing else will happen."

Gabe jumps in. "But if she *has* already registered, you might find her information right away and be able to start a request to get in touch."

My heart is pounding so hard in my chest that I'm finding it difficult to breathe. *Stop it*, I tell myself. Odds are that she hasn't ever signed up for these registries. And what if I think I've found my daughter, but it's just another scammer? I don't think I could bear to go through that again.

"Or you could hire a private eye, but that's probably super expensive."

"No," I say, "I don't want to go to those lengths. I'm not even sure I want to look at the websites you're talking about."

"Of course. I understand, *Gramasoda*," Ethan says. "But would it be okay if I just email over the links to you?"

He's gone to all this trouble. "That's fine, Ethan. And thank you for taking the time to do all that research." Even if I never use any of it.

We wrap up our call with promises to talk regularly. Such caring and considerate young men. I feel honored to be their *sorta* Grandma.

Chapter 28

It's been a disappointing morning. Ruth and I have just driven well over an hour to locate the trailhead for a wonderful-sounding hike she discovered online, only to find that the trail is closed due to a rockslide about a quarter mile in. With no cell service and no detailed printed map for the immediate area, we're at a loss for where else to hike today, now that we've driven this far.

"How about we drive back to where we saw those cars parked just off the highway," she says. "That might have been a trailhead."

We climb back into my Jeep and turn back the way we came. After about ten minutes, we locate the spot and pull in beside a lone pickup truck in the small parking area. None of the other cars we saw earlier are still around, but sure enough, there's a sign by an obvious pathway – "Ehrlich Trail."

"A trail named after you. It's an omen!" I say.

"Except they didn't spell Erlich correctly. So it's not an omen," she says with a glint in her eye. "It's a *sign*." She stares at me as if expecting something. "Get it? A sign? A trail sign?"

I moan. "I must be slipping." Franklin was the ultimate

punster, but without him in my life, I'm no longer quick at recognizing one.

Snickering, she starts along the trail and I follow. After just a few minutes, we reach a large, wooden platform where a tall, lanky man probably in his seventies stands looking out at the view. He nods at us as we move to the railing, then returns his attention to the scenery.

Saguaro cactus reach spindly arms high into the sky in the foreground and rugged, rocky peaks jut up from the desert floor. A distinctive, pointed spire stands out in the distance, reminding me of the nib of a fountain pen. "Do you know what that one is called?" I ask the man, pointing toward the horizon.

"That's Weaver's Needle," he says. "I've climbed it. But that was a few years back."

Ruth's face lights up. "Ellie, maybe we can hike up it."

"Um, are you ladies experienced rock climbers?" he asks. When we shake our heads, he continues, "Because it's generally considered a 'technical climb' where you use ropes and harnesses."

"Oh. Too bad," Ruth says. Inwardly, I sigh in relief. "Maybe we could just hike up closer to it?"

"Sure," he says. "There's a good trail you can use to circle the peak, but that's pretty long, maybe twelve or thirteen miles with a lot of elevation gain. Or you can just hike to a saddle where you'll get great views of the Needle. That's more like six miles and 1,500 feet of gain."

Which isn't trivial, but is a distance I feel capable of managing, now that I've proven myself on that trail in the North Cascades.

Before he leaves, I make a note of the trail he's recommended so I can research more details when we get back to camp. Meanwhile, it dawns on us that we've reached the end of *this* trail. I doubt if it was even a quarter mile to this point. Even at a leisurely pace, we'll be back at our car before ten

A.M., which leaves a lot of time in the day and no real plan.

Ruth and I roll down the windows and sit in the SUV after our walk, trying to come up with something else to do with ourselves. It seems a shame to head all the way back to camp after having driven all this way, and we didn't think to ask the gentleman about other hikes in this area. The trail he described to us starts on the opposite side of Weaver's Needle, so that's much too far away to consider today.

"Are you hungry?" I ask, remembering a funky little café we passed earlier this morning. It had a sign out front, *Breakfast All Day*. Suddenly, I have a tremendous craving for an omelet.

"I suppose I could be," she says. "What do you have in mind?"

"Second breakfast." I remind her of the diner and we set off, hoping we don't discover the place is closed on Sundays.

Omelet, omelet, omelet my stomach chants as I drive. There's only one car in the parking lot, but they're open!

"Only one other car? That's not a good sign," Ruth says, and this time she's not referring to the *Breakfast All Day* notice.

"It's 10:30 – probably in between their breakfast and lunch crowds. Anyway, it's hard to mess up pancakes and eggs. I'm still game. What do you say?"

"It's worth a shot," she says.

The screen door squeaks loudly as we step inside. "Just sit anywhere," a young woman wearing an apron calls out from the entrance to the kitchen. "I'll be right with you." She steps away from the man she was talking to in the back and fetches some menus.

The other car in the lot must belong to her or the cook, since there are no other customers in the place. We select a table by the front window and she hands us the menus, simple lists printed on plain office paper. "Coffee?" she asks, nodding at the empty cups on the table. We both smile and say, "Yes, please," in unison.

I study the section of the menu labeled *Breakfast*. They have scrambled eggs, either plain or "deluxe" with onions and peppers. Buttermilk pancakes. French toast. All with a choice of bacon or sausage and either toast or hash browns. No omelets – damn! My heart is set on an omelet. I don't even care what's in it. Surely their chef can modify his or her routine just a wee bit and cook up eggs in the form of an omelet instead of scrambled.

When our waitress – Amber, according to her nametag – returns to fill our cups, I ask if that's possible. "Can I have an omelet with the onions and peppers instead of scrambled eggs? And maybe add some Swiss cheese?" The lunch menu lists Swiss, American, and cheddar options for their burgers, so clearly they have some on hand.

"What's an omelet?" she asks.

Ruth and I exchange a glance and I try not to look at Amber like she's nuts. How can someone who works in a place that serves an all-day breakfast not know what an omelet is?

"Well, it's similar to scrambled eggs," I say. "But instead of scrambling the egg mixture, you just cook it flat."

She frowns and squints her eyes, clearly puzzled. "Scrambled, but flat?"

I don't see any point in describing the preparation steps further. "I'm sure your cook will know how to fix it. Can you please just ask him if he can cook me an omelet with the peppers and onion, and add Swiss cheese? I'll have bacon and whole wheat toast with that."

"Okay," she says, scribbling on her pad. "Except we don't have whole wheat. Only white. Is that okay?"

Ruth's instincts about this place were probably right, but this isn't a deal breaker. "That'll be all right. White toast."

Amber takes Ruth's order of pancakes and sausage. "No

bread or potatoes, please," confuses her briefly, but once Ruth confirms that she only wants the two items and nothing else, Amber looks more confident.

"I'll get your order in right away," she says, heading for the kitchen. Since there's nobody else here, I would certainly hope that's the case.

We've only been chatting for a few minutes when our waitress emerges from the kitchen carrying two plates of steaming food. Their short-order cook is fast. Now let's see how he did on my omelet.

Amber sets down Ruth's plate first and the pancakes are perfect, golden brown and fluffy. The bacon is crispy and still sizzling. My mouth waters in anticipation of my lovely omelet. Then she places my plate on the table, smiles broadly, and trots back to the kitchen.

"What *is* that?" Ruth asks.

I think the blob covering my plate may once have been scrambled eggs with veggies. It appears that they've been smashed into a flat, broad disk, with a moist square of Swiss cheese floating over the center of the circle. It resembles a pale yellow Frisbee with green spots and a post-it note stuck to the middle. It seems the cook doesn't know what an omelet is, either.

"I'm not sure," I say, but venture to slice off a bite with my fork and give it a try. It's edible, but doesn't resemble any omelet I've ever eaten. I'm disappointed, but hungry enough to finish it off. "I think it's scrambled eggs that have been crushed under an iron skillet."

When Amber presents the tab, Ruth insists it's her turn to buy. She studies the check for a moment, then bursts out laughing.

"What?"

"Take a look," she says, passing the paper over to me.

Amber has written *Deluxe scrambled eggs, FLAT* !!!!

"Looks like the cook made exactly what Amber asked for," she says, and we both burst out laughing.

***

For almost a week now, I've toyed with actually exploring the website links that Ethan sent me. I should just forget about the whole thing, like I did for years. I'll explain to Ruth and the boys that I've decided not to search for my daughter, and would they please accept my decision and not raise the matter again, thank you very much.

Who am I kidding? The truth is that I'd love to develop a connection to my only child. I'd love to show off photos of my grandchildren to everyone I meet. But I'm afraid of having my heart stomped upon again. Even if I find my real daughter, there's no guarantee we'll hit it off. Maybe she resents me for giving her away. What if she's not a very nice person?

Despite all that, there's a part of me that needs to know.

Choosing one at random, I click a link that Ethan provided and read the information on the website. *This is nuts.* He cautioned me that the odds are slim that my daughter is also searching for me, so nothing is likely to come of this.

With great trepidation, I create a free account, entering my maiden name, the date I gave birth, and the name of the hospital. It prompts me for the address, but when I search for Midwest Oasis General Hospital in Vanderwal, Iowa, there's no such name anymore. Scanning an online map of the town for current hospitals proves useless – I just can't remember much about the exact location of the hospital 47 years ago, and the town appears to have grown significantly since then. I leave that line blank.

Holding my breath, I click *Search*. A list of several usernames comes up, but as I scan the details beside each one, there's no match to Vanderwal, although all list Iowa as their birthplace. Two show August 13 as a date of birth, which is correct, but they have the wrong year. My daughter isn't in the database.

Willing to give it one more shot, I select another website that Ethan provided and go through the process again. This time, the search results are presented differently, with a score beside each line. Three people have been rated at 90% or above, meaning there's at least a 90% chance that they are a good match. But I have to sign up for an annual membership to learn more about any of them. Cautiously, I begin the process of upgrading to the premium level, determined to learn the cost before I actually provide my credit card information. When I discover that I must pay $249 to learn if any of the three so-called matches might really be my child, I bookmark the web page and close down my browser. If I knew for certain that I'd be connecting with my kin, I might consider paying that much. Then again, I've already flushed $8,000 down the drain – why throw good money after bad?

Frustrated, I put away my laptop and fetch my e-reader, determined to immerse myself in the story of two sisters who have inherited their great aunt's secluded cabin in the backwoods of Maine. The next chapter may reveal whether they encounter Sasquatch, a mysterious child raised by wolves, a hermit who's been looking for love in all the wrong places, a serial killer recently escaped from death row, or an extraterrestrial. I'm rooting for a handsome hermit with a twin brother.

Chapter 29

We're settled into our spots in an RV Village smack in the middle of metropolitan Phoenix. Desert Sunset RV and MH Resort covers a broad expanse of land, with most of the area devoted to Mobile Homes, tiny houses that could, in theory, be moved, but seem so well established with decking, attached awnings, and tiny gardens that I doubt any of them will ever be "mobile" again. Ruth and I are camped in the RV section toward the back of the property. Although they've made an effort to plant palm trees and bushes between the campsites, the area still reminds me of a giant parking lot. Oh well. There's so much to do in the big city that we'll seldom be hanging around outside our campers. And the cost for our three-month reservations is delightfully low.

Daily, we can choose among an assortment of classes and activities organized within Desert Sunset, or opt to leave the resort to visit a museum, attend a concert, enjoy a festival, browse a farmer's market, or do what we love the best – hike. After spending the majority of our time far from any large populated areas, I'm feeling culture shock here in a big city. It's tempting to go out to eat all the time, but we've sworn to limit restaurant visits to just one or two per week.

This afternoon, I've opted to find out if swimming is like riding a bicycle – once you learn how, it comes back to you quickly. It's been years since I last swam a lap, but with an on-site Olympic-length pool available just a five-minute walk from my camper, it seems like I should give it a shot. There were a number of years when I wouldn't have been caught dead wearing something that revealed my body shape, but I'm feeling much better about myself now, so being seen in a swim suit doesn't horrify me like it once did. Okay, so I'm a bit thicker through the waist, saggy, and the skin on my legs looks like crepe paper. I'm not twenty anymore. Who cares?

The pool is outdoors, but there's a huge "sail" hung above the entire area for shade. The resort manager told me they'll be taking it down for the winter, but not until Thanksgiving, later this month. Having grown up in Denver, I can't get over how hot it still gets here in November.

After only a half dozen laps, I'm feeling tired. Isn't it amazing how I can feel like I'm in great shape for one activity, but discover I've got a long way to go when I try something different? I fetch a large inflated ring from the supply of pool gear and prop my upper body inside the circle so I can float lazily around the deep end. Remarkably, I'm the only person actually getting into the water. Two older ladies are sitting in chairs on the deck, chatting and knitting.

My mind keeps drifting back to the whole reunion thing. It's been almost two weeks since I entered my information on the two search websites. As expected, nothing else has come of the free site that didn't find any matches, and I haven't convinced myself to pay what I consider to be an unreasonable fee to learn if the other site actually contains useful information, or if that's just another come-on to drain my money.

Just let it go, I tell myself.

But, what if she's been looking for me? If I were adopted,

wouldn't I want to learn more about my natural parents, even if only to have medical information that could be helpful?

Suddenly noticing that the two knitters are staring at me, I realize that I've been muttering my thoughts out loud. Great – I'm a crazy lady who argues with herself while floating in the pool. I smile and nod at them before kicking over to the shallow end so I can retreat before they call someone to take me away in a straightjacket.

Back in the women's locker room, I step into one of the shower cubicles. There's a small area for dressing with a miniscule bench. I can never figure out where to put my shower bag and clothes in these places. Only two wall hooks? If I hang my towel where I can reach it, that leaves only one hook for my clean shirt, pants, key ring, sunglasses, underwear, and bra.

Somehow I find a spot for everything, deciding that I can remove my swimsuit once I'm in the shower and hang it from the soap dish. I turn on the water and adjust the temperature, holding the shower curtain as closed as possible so the spray doesn't reach my dry clothes. Pulling back the curtain to step inside, my eye catches movement.

I emit a high-pitched whimper and leap back from the shower stall, fumble with the cubicle door lock, and race out of the locker room.

"There's a tarantula in the shower!" I shriek repeatedly, scurrying down the hall to the front desk of the resort's clubhouse. Goosebumps cover my arms and legs – partly from the frigid air conditioning on my wet swimsuit but possibly due to the shock of discovering the monstrous spider.

"There's a tarantula in the shower!" I declare again to the woman sitting at the desk, as if she wouldn't have heard me shouting as I approached.

She smiles and nods her head, as if I had just commented on the pretty flowers blooming on the cactus outside the door. "We get them now and then. They're really quite harmless."

The scene from the movie *Annie Hall* pops into my mind. Annie tells her boyfriend that there's a spider in her bathtub. He goes in to kill it, but immediately retreats, declaring, "There's a spider in your bathroom the size of a Buick!"

"Harmless?" I say to her. "It's as big as a dinner plate!" Which *isn't* an exaggeration.

She pushes back her rolling chair and stands. "Let's go take a look."

I follow her back to the shower area, but stand well back from the confining area of the cubicle. She disappears within and I hear the water shut off. I'll probably get in trouble for leaving the shower running.

Moments later, here she comes with Godzilla the Tarantula crawling slowly along her outstretched arm. Somehow, I manage to suppress a scream, but I do emit a high-pitched whimper. When the creature reaches her elbow, she offers it her other hand to step onto and transfers it to that side.

"Isn't she beautiful?" she says. "Would you like to hold her?"

Nope, nope, nope! "I think I'll pass," I say, backing farther away and pressing myself against the wall. As she turns to take her hairy, eight-legged buddy outside, I call out my thanks and return to the shower stall. This time, I throw back the curtain and examine the area thoroughly, then repeat the process with the other showers in the row and all the toilet stalls before I'm willing to continue.

Lucky thing I hadn't already removed my swimsuit before spotting that beast, or I might have staged a replay of that time Ruth and I ran naked through the woods.

As I get dressed, I make a decision. I'll continue what I started and try out the remaining web links that Ethan sent me. My daughter deserves to get her questions answered — assuming she is looking for me.

Back home, in front of my laptop, the next website I try is similar to the free one, except it finds one female born on the right date in Iowa, but the specific location is unknown. This could be it! If I want to send her a message, I must sign up for a paid account, but this time I have the option of only spending $5.99 for a one-month membership, which I can cancel before it renews. As I always do, I double-check that I'm on a secure website before entering my credit card details, and I set a reminder on my calendar to be sure to manually cancel my account in a month, since otherwise they'll automatically charge me again.

There – done!

My hands trembling, I type out a message to *Chanelle*, my possible daughter. *Chanelle* – what a pretty name!

Dear Chanelle,

You might be my daughter! I was 16 when I gave birth at Midwest Oasis Hospital in Vanderwal, Iowa on August 13, 1973.

To the best of my recollection, my daughter weighed 5 pounds, 10 ounces at birth and was born 3 weeks early. I would have named her Donna if my circumstances were different and I could have raised her myself.

I re-read what I've written and decide to delete the last sentence, afraid it might be off-putting. What if she resented that I gave her up, even though I was so young? I don't want to assume anything.

For several more minutes, I try out different ways to end my note, finally settling on:

I'm very much looking forward to hearing from you and pray that you are, indeed, my daughter.

Hopefully yours,
Ellie

Too personal? Not if she's my child, it's not! After all, Chanelle went through the same thing I'm doing – going online to search for her natural family. She *wants* to connect.

I send the message and sit staring at my computer. How soon will she see my note? Will she reply immediately? Is Chanelle my real daughter?

A familiar tap on my door interrupts my nervous fretting, and I call out for Ruth to come in. She's wearing the cat draped around her neck.

"How was your spin class?" I ask. I've never been much of a bicyclist, myself, so the idea of peddling a stationary bike in unison with a roomful of people while an instructor shouts *Let's go! Pick it up! Woo hoo!* sounds like a torture session to me.

"It was a blast! Our instructor put on some really lively music and encouraged us to move our bodies like we were dancing while spinning."

Maybe I can sneak into the back next time and take a video.

"I'm going for a stroll through the rich part of town," she says. "Want to join me?"

That's our little joke here in Desert Sunset – there's a section of the resort with modest-sized modular homes which we've declared to be the "rich" neighborhood. Another area with the smaller mobile homes is "the hood," while our RV camping section is for us "trailer trash." All in jest, of course. There are folks in each of the resort regions who are quite wealthy as well as those who are barely scraping by.

Strolling around the grounds with my best friend and a darling cat always manages to help me clear my mind. I almost insist on turning around when I realize I left my phone behind, but resolve to let it be. I'd rather be inside my camper when Chanelle sends a reply than out here, squinting at my phone screen in the bright sunlight, trying to make out what she's written.

Abruptly, my thoughts are interrupted by the frantic barking and snarling of a small dog, barely restrained by a low fence in the tiny yard of a miniature house. His entire body jerks with each loud bark and I'm afraid he'll leap the fence at any moment. Charli squirms franticly and bounds to the ground from Ruth's shoulders, landing in a posture that screams out *ready for battle*. She hisses and emits a chilling moan, her fur standing on end so she appears to have tripled in size.

The dog takes a few steps back, the tempo of his barks slowing dramatically. Charli doubles down on her eerie moans and inches forward, eyes locked on her adversary like a demon's. He manages one more *yelp* which sounds like it is more of a question than an angry shout, turns sideways while keeping an eye on the cat, then bounds away to the relative safety of the house's front porch. He watches Charli carefully, exhaling a timid bark now and then.

"Charli, come on," Ruth calls, reaching for her. The cat issues one final hiss in the direction of her opponent, then allows her mom to pick her up. We hurry away, both petting and speaking to Charli in our most comforting voices. Her fur settles back into place and she's transformed back into the sweet, gentle pussycat we know and love.

"Kind of reminds you of The Exorcist, doesn't she?" Ruth says, nuzzling the cat's soft coat. "She can turn her head around so it's almost facing backward, and everyone knows about cats hacking up fur balls."

I scratch Charli behind her ear and she purrs loudly.

"Don't worry, little one. Your mom didn't really mean it."

Ruth raises an eyebrow and points to a long scratch across the back of her arm. "Yes I did. But I still love her."

When we arrive back at our sites, I snatch up my phone to check for messages. My pulse speeds up when I spot the email notification from the reunion site and I click on the link to retrieve Chanelle's note.

Hello Ellie,

I have the modified birth certificate they issued after I was adopted, and it says I weighed 8 lbs. 11 oz. but perhaps one of our numbers is simply an error.

I was told that my mother was in her mid 20s when she had me. Her husband had just been killed in Vietnam and she already had two children, one with special needs. She was barely getting by and didn't think she could manage another child.

Please let me know if this still sounds like you are my mother.

Chanelle

My body feels like it has just deflated. Even in her brief message, I pick up on Chanelle's pessimism about the two of us being a match. Disappointed, I fire off a quick response wishing her success in her continued search.

Do I try again with another adoption database? Or go back to plan A – try to forget all about this? *Can* I forget again?

Chapter 30

A blood-curling scream stops us in our tracks.

"Did you see it? Did it come this way?" The woman sounds frantic and is rushing toward us on the path in the city park we're visiting. Her eyes opened wide, she spins around, searching for whatever "it" is that has her in such turmoil.

"It was chasing me!" she says, a tremor in her voice. "Turn back – don't go on."

Not waiting to see if we heed her warning, she dashes away.

Ruth and I look at each other. "What do you think?" I say. "Should we turn around?"

We stare at the path ahead, searching for a hint of movement of the *thing* that was chasing her. I inch forward and squint into the bushes and plants along the edge of the packed gravel trail. Nothing.

"Let's go on," Ruth says. "We'll just keep our eyes open. I can't imagine what she might have seen here in the middle of the city."

"That ear-splitting shriek probably scared it off," I say, trying to convince myself. I'm so glad I didn't scream like that when I encountered the tarantula in the shower. I made enough of a fool of myself as it is.

We walk slowly, scanning both sides of the path, and considering possible answers to what frightened the woman so badly.

"A tarantula. Or one of those things that kind of looks like a pig but isn't," I say.

"That's a javelina – have you ever seen one up close? They look kind of scary. Or maybe it was a rattlesnake."

"Or a coyote."

"A prairie dog," she offers and we chuckle. Whatever it was, we're not seeing anything.

"A bunny rabbit."

"A pigeon."

"A pterodactyl."

"A guy wearing a dinosaur costume."

Something emerges from the brush and I gasp, frozen in place. "Oh my God. What *is* that?"

A strange primitive-looking creature halts in the middle of the track, spins its head toward us and a long, black tongue shoots out of its mouth, then is swiftly pulled back. It appears to be a lizard, but nothing like any I've seen before while hiking in the desert, and I've spotted plenty of them. They've ranged from about two inches in length to perhaps six. They're incredibly quick, many are colorful, and I've found all of them adorable. Sometimes I've come across a cute little gecko perched on a rock and watched as it performed push-ups on its tiny little front legs, as if showing off its fitness. Others have lifted their colorful heads high when I've aimed my phone camera at them, presenting their best pose.

This giant is close to two feet long with a body thicker than my arm. There's a black and orange-ish pattern all along its back and tail. Its legs and body resemble a baby crocodile's, but its head reminds me more of a snake. It watches us with beady eyes, flicking its tongue at us repeatedly. It steps backward, distancing itself from us in slow motion, and I'm startled to see its multiple toes sheathed with nasty-looking claws.

"Isn't that amazing?" Ruth says, leaning over to get a closer look. "I think it's a Gila Monster."

Monster is an appropriate name for this beast. I can understand that woman's initial fright when she spotted it, yet it seems slow-moving and wary of us. I'm more fascinated than frightened, but I fully intend to give it space – an option that was difficult in a small shower stall, but easily achieved out here. I take a couple of photos, zooming in for details, before it waddles slowly back into the underbrush and disappears from sight.

"That was pretty cool," I say.

"I'm still holding out for a pterodactyl," Ruth says as we resume our stroll in the park.

***

Ethan sent me an email asking how my search is going. Do I inform him that I'm giving up because it's too stressful and nothing has come of it? Or do I wait until I've tried out the final two websites and then tell him?

I feel guilty for the effort he put into researching this for me, so I decide to bite the bullet and get the final disappointments out of the way. Knowing those sites are out there is holding me back from forgetting this whole affair. I'm not going to find my daughter and the authorities are not going to catch "Lisa" and I need to move on.

With as much enthusiasm as I have when filling out my income tax returns, I provide answers to the questions on the page on the state of Iowa's website. After submitting the information, a box informs me that it will take at least ten days to return any results. Kind of a "Don't call us, we'll call you" message. I don't hold out any hope that will pan out.

The final site is very similar to the others I've tried. When a "match" to my limited information is listed, I shake my head, staving off any glimmer of optimism. Should I even bother sending a note to this person? What the heck – let's get this over with.

This time around, I compose the message quickly, simply repeating what I said to Chanelle, but I tone down the closing lines to read:

I'm looking forward to hearing from you.

Ellie

I send it off to the stranger who shares a birthday with my daughter and sigh with relief. That's finished. I've respected Ethan's efforts, but they didn't pan out. It's all for the best. During the early days after hearing from my fake daughter, I got online and read about reunions between adoptees and their real mothers. Some were wonderful stories but others were heartbreaking, saying "I wish I had never contacted her." My little melodrama with "Lisa" played out like a fairy tale, complete with a daughter I could "save" and two wonderful grandchildren to cherish. But that's all it was – a fairy tale. In real life, my daughter may resent me and only want contact so she can answer some long-time questions. Or she may not be the smart, accomplished woman I dream she might be. Maybe we wouldn't even like each other.

I shut my laptop and put it away. Done! All behind me. Time to move on.

And then my phone *pings* with a message.

Chapter 31

The woman in the photo could be me from fifteen years ago, the resemblance is so strong. Unless this is an elaborate scheme to Photoshop an old picture of me, there is no longer any doubt in my mind that this person, Dana Blankenship, is my daughter. Her complexion is a few shades darker than mine and she has Tony's dark brown eyes and nearly black hair, but otherwise she could be my twin.

She's the real deal!

I reply to her message with an image of myself posing by Crater Lake, and ask her to call me. She replies,

> **How about a video call? After all these years of waiting to meet you, I can hardly wait to talk face to face. That would be the next best thing.**

I answer,

> **That's a great idea, but I don't know how to set it up on my phone.**

She assures me that it's simple and describes what I should do when she calls. Waiting anxiously, I answer the ring immediately. My daughter's face fills the screen and lights up. My smile is so huge that my cheek muscles ache.

"Hi, Ellie. I'm so thrilled to finally meet you!"

Tears fill my eyes and her image blurs. I swipe them away and try to speak, but my throat is so tight I can't say a word.

She tears up, too. "I know. It's pretty amazing, isn't it? Did you ever imagine we would look so much alike? I look *nothing* like my parents – sorry, my adoptive parents."

I manage to get my voice back. "No need to be sorry. They *are* your parents. I don't feel slighted." I turn away from the phone and blow my nose. "I'm going to dig up a picture of me from when I was about your age and send it to you. At first, I thought you'd sent me my own photo."

We talk for almost an hour, taking turns asking question after question. Dana explains that she first registered for the reunion search site six years ago. "I felt determined to locate you before I turned fifty," she says. "I beat my goal by almost three years!"

I decide to dive right in and ask the hardest question: "How do you feel about me for giving you up for adoption?"

"Well, I can't say that I was always okay with that," she says, frowning slightly. "Especially when I was in those pre-teen and early teen years, I didn't understand why you made that choice. I saw it as a personal rejection – that you didn't think I was good enough."

"Oh, Dana, I'm so sorry you felt that way. It's just that I was—"

"No, no – it's okay. When I got old enough to understand that *I* could become pregnant and to really try to imagine what it would be like to have a baby that young, that totally changed my perspective. Now, I can't say that I didn't assume that I was *so* much more mature and worldly than you had been," she says, her voice imitating that of a haughty teenager. "So if I had become pregnant, I would surely have raised the baby myself. Ha!" she laughs. "I just needed a few more years under my belt before I recognized how naïve I had been!"

We both chuckle at that.

The conversation turns to her family. Her parents, Sheila and Forrest, live nearby, and they get together for dinner every Sunday night at Dana's house.

"And where is home?" I ask.

"Denver. My folks moved here from Iowa when I was ten."

"Denver? I grew up in Denver!" I say, marveling that we might have walked right by one another and not realized it. Then again, since I moved to California with Franklin not long after we married, Dana and I may not have been in Colorado at the same time.

I learn that she is married to Adam, a nurse practitioner at a large Family Practice, and their daughter, Mia, is a college sophomore at the University of Colorado in Boulder. Another crazy coincidence – my alma mater!

As we continue talking, we discover more in common. Dana also went to CU, majoring in journalism, and she writes for a regional magazine, which is remarkably similar to my early career. Our favorite color is blue, favorite food is "anything chocolate," and we both enjoy gardening. She loves to hike and go backpacking, having done both from an early age with her parents, while I came to enjoy outdoor activities only recently, thanks to Ruth's influence.

But she loves football ("Go Broncos!") while I don't follow any major sports. I've rediscovered the pleasure of swimming, yet she'll go out of her way to avoid the water. She's crazy about country music and going out dancing, while I prefer folk rock and hate to dance.

When we've both started to lose our voices, we reluctantly

wind up the call. "Can I call you again on Sunday night?" she asks. "That way I can introduce you to the rest of the family."

"How are they going to feel about that?" I ask, thinking mainly of her parents. Dana is so enthusiastic about connecting with me. Won't her father, and especially her mother, resent that? Yes, I get credit for carrying her for close to nine months and going through hours of labor, but they've been there for her for the past forty-seven years while I did my best to forget she even exists.

"Don't worry," she says. "We've talked about the possibility of meeting you for most of my life. They've always been supportive of my questions about you and wanting to find you."

Still, being supportive in theory may not pan out to what happens when the real thing comes their way. "Talk it over with everyone first. We have the rest of our lives to figure out these new relationships, Dana. If they need more time, that's not a problem."

"Fair enough," she says. "I'll text you to let you know what's going on. Even if we decide to wait on the big introduction, I'd still like for you and me to talk again."

"Absolutely!" I say, looking straight into her eyes on my camera display. "Dana, I'm so glad you wanted to find me. I can tell already that you've become an accomplished, warm, and caring woman and I'm so, so proud of you." Oh, dear – here come the happy tears again.

"And I'm thrilled that you are such a loving, brave woman, Ellie. I'm looking forward to visiting again soon."

The moment the call disconnects, I dash out my door and head over to Ruth's place to share my big news. When my phone *pings*, I snatch it from my pocket and beam when I realize that my daughter has sent me a batch of photos. After taking a moment to view the first one – a shot of a young Dana hiking with an enormous backpack and an even larger smile on her face – I decide to wait and view the rest along with my best friend. I can manage to wait another thirty seconds, can't I?

Chapter 32

Waiting for Sunday night to roll around feels like anticipating the first time Franklin took me to meet his parents back when we were dating. That was over forty years ago, but I remember it all too well. I was so worked up, I couldn't even think about breakfast before we were setting out to go visit them. Franklin tried to get me to eat a snack during our drive, but I was sure I wouldn't be able to keep anything down. By the time we arrived, I think my blood sugar level had plummeted. We walked up to their front door and I passed out cold on the porch! What a way to make a good first impression. As it turned out, that actually seemed to endear them to me — especially Franklin's mom — since our first interaction was for them to fuss over me and nurse me back to health with a scrumptious meal.

I'm excited about talking with my genuine granddaughter, Mia, for the first time, but nervous about being introduced to Dana's adoptive parents. Not so nervous that I can't eat, though. Fainting during a video call would probably not win over her parents, especially since nobody on that end of the call would understand why my phone's camera is providing an extreme close up view of the floor or why I've suddenly stopped speaking to them.

I figure it would be smart to tone down the whole "grandma" bit. From what Dana has already told me, her folks have been quite involved in Mia's life, regularly babysitting her after school and some weekdays during the summer when she was little, and still sharing Sunday dinners once or twice a month when Mia drives the short distance from Boulder to Denver to see her family. Unlike that fictitious granddaughter – the one who sounded *exactly* like her fake mother on the phone, *surprise, surprise* – Mia is close to her entire extended family. She has real grandparents – two sets! – who have been part of her life since the day she was born. I'm the fake, the intruder.

Meanwhile, I make sure my mind is kept busy. I join the resort's book club and rush to read their latest choice in time for the discussion early next week. Ruth and I hike up some of the hills located right in the midst of the city, opting for early starts since the days are still rather hot by afternoon, despite it being mid-November. If I'm not too tired when we return to camp, I swim. In the evening, after dinner, we stroll around and visit with the people we encounter sitting outside their camper or their tiny house.

Sunday evening finally arrives and I've managed to eat a light dinner with Ruth before excusing myself and heading back to my place to wait for my phone to ring. No fainting.

When the call connects, I feel a shudder of joy as my daughter's face comes into view. "Hi, Ellie," Dana says. "Everybody's here and looking forward to meeting you."

A man's head tilts over and presses close to hers. "Hi," he says as she adjusts the angle of the camera to show both of their faces, "I'm Adam. My wife is over the moon about finding you – that's all she's talked about all week. It's great to finally meet you." He is even better looking than in the pictures she sent me – strong jawline and a gorgeous smile. I admit I wasn't expecting that her husband would be African American, but once I saw photos of Dana with Adam and their daughter, I felt great joy. Their love for one another is undeniable, and that's been one of my greatest hopes – that my child would have a life filled with loving relationships.

"I'm so pleased that Dana and I have finally connected, and it's a pleasure to meet you as well." *Relax*, I tell myself, *don't be so formal.*

The view spins to Dana's left. "And here's our daughter, Mia."

"Hey," she says, sounding even more nervous than I am. Her smile looks forced. "Nice to meet you, um..." – she pauses, eyes flicking toward her parents – "...um, Mrs. Dwyer."

Her pitch rises at the end, making it sound like a question. "You can call me Ellie," I say, "or, if you want—" I don't finish. She and Dana are exchanging glances, Mia with a touch of panic in her eyes. I can almost hear them recounting an earlier discussion about how to address me. I can't guess the details, but I'm pretty sure at least one person in that room isn't comfortable with her calling me "Grandma" or any variation of that endearing term.

"So, yeah. Ellie." She's run out of things to say.

"It's great to meet you, Mia. I understand you're majoring in communication and media studies at CU. Did your mother tell you that I went there as well?"

"Yeah. That's pretty cool."

Dana swings the camera back to her face. "Let me introduce you to my parents, Sheila and Forrest Linscott. Here we go..."

With a dizzying scan of the room, two new faces come into focus. Dana's adoptive parents both have a Nordic look about them – very light complexions and blue eyes. Sheila Linscott has pale blond hair, which I'm guessing is dyed, but close to her original shade. Forrest Linscott is totally bald, with thick, white eyebrows. Judging by the way he's leaning over to place his face close to his wife's, I think he's quite tall.

"Hello, Ellie," Forrest says, and Sheila echoes him. "So pleased to meet you." His smile is open and warm, but her lips are pressed tightly together, a smile so strained I fear her face might crack.

"This is so wonderful." I've been thinking about what I wanted to express to them and hope it will convey enough. "My deepest hope has always been that my baby would grow up in a loving home, and everything I've learned this past week and tonight has reassured me that she ended up with exactly the right family. I can't begin to express my gratitude to you for being Dana's parents and all that entails."

Forrest grasps his wife's shoulders and gives her a supportive squeeze. "Ellie, we thank you for bringing this delightful, beautiful, loving person into the world so she could be in our lives. She has brought us more joy than words can possibly express."

Sheila's face relaxes ever so slightly. "Thank you," she whispers. I pause before speaking, hoping she might say more, but she remains silent, reaching for her husband's hand and nodding at Dana, signaling that her promised task is now complete.

"Well, that's everybody!" Dana says in a too-bright voice, focusing her camera on herself. "Let's visit again later in the week, Ellie – just you and me."

Thank heavens *she* still wants to get better acquainted. We sign off, with a chorus of unseen voices calling out, "Goodbye, Ellie" as the call ends.

Well, there you go. Reality often doesn't coincide with fairy tales. But I'm okay with this. Perhaps more of the family will become comfortable with my insertion in their lives over time, or not. Dana may reach a point where she knows all that she wants to know about me, and no longer reaches out. That would be sad, but I still feel like something wonderful has happened here. My infant found a better life than she would have had with an immature, single mother who would have had to drop out of high school. Maybe my parents would have helped, but not without casting a pall of shame over me and my baby. No, that wouldn't have been a loving, supportive environment. I did the right thing.

Chapter 33

The Thanksgiving gathering here at Desert Sunset was quite festive. Management provided the roast turkeys, while everyone who attended the event brought all the fixings. I recreated the jelled cranberry salad I like so much – other than the time it oozed all over my camper floor when my refrigerator came open while I was towing. Ruth contributed a gorgeous tossed salad and we could barely find space on the long serving tables to place our offerings. I thought there was far more food than the crowd of about eighty could possibly eat, but we certainly came close!

That was a week ago and I'm still trying to get enough exercise to burn off all those calories. Fortunately, Ruth is more than happy to help me discover places to hike to achieve my goal. Her latest discovery is geocaching. She consults a map on her phone that discloses where objects have been hidden and we go treasure hunting using our phones' GPS tracking to locate the approximate spot for one of the caches. When we discover one – or more accurately, *if* we find it, since the items can be quite small and extremely well hidden – we get to sign a register (usually) choose a "treasure" from the box, then leave our own item for the next person. We soon learn that many of the goodies are mainly of interest to children – small, plastic toys or colorful stickers – so we don't generally remove any of the items. Today, we found one geocache just off a trail to a dry waterfall, but have been stumped when searching for another close to the turn-around point. Still, it's fun and some of the points we've explored have taken us to places we might not have discovered otherwise.

When we return to Desert Sunset, I realize there's a voicemail waiting for me from Maxwell, my bank contact about the Fraud investigation. He asks me to call him back.

"There's been an arrest," he tells me. "We believe this individual was involved in a significant number of scams similar to what you experienced. She managed to stay one step ahead of the authorities for a while, but didn't switch banks quickly enough this last time around. Last week, we were able to link two large fund transfers connected to other reported scams that were deposited into a recently-opened account. I can't go into details, but authorities were able to convince her to return to the bank in person to withdraw the target funds, and were able to apprehend her at that time."

Wow. The only other information that I'm able to extract from Maxwell is that my money is probably irretrievable and that they may need me to testify at a future trial. Or not. "We already have your written statement and copies of all your correspondence with the suspect," he explains. "We'll be in touch if anything else is needed, but that's unlikely. We're focusing on the larger transactions at this point."

I wonder how much money Fake Lisa stole from all her targets. Maxwell's statements lead me to believe my $8,000 was small change within the big picture.

Since Ethan was so much a part of spotting the red flags and extracting me from a financial disaster, I call him to pass along the news. "Let me see if I can dig up any more information," he says as Gabe calls out in the background,

"Way to go, dude! You helped them crack the case!"

I see no reason to burst his bubble. Ethan's still my hero for saving me from losing far more money.

Less than an hour later, as Ruth and I are preparing dinner, Ethan calls back. "I found some more information," he says. "They arrested Malorie Thunderburk, a.k.a. Malorie Burke, a.k.a. Lorie Burke, a,k.a. Malorie Thunder, at a bank in Dallas, Texas."

That's a lot of aliases. Fake Lisa has been one busy scammer.

"She's 32 years old and has several prior convictions, including running the classic 'Grandparent scam' along with a partner-in-crime, Theodore 'Junkyard' Festel, who is serving a six-year term for wire fraud and grand larceny. She got out early due to a plea bargain."

"I've heard of the Grandparent scam," I tell him. Obviously, if I had received a phone call out of the blue from someone claiming to be my grandchild, desperate for bail money or funds to pay for emergency medical care, I would never have fallen for it. I didn't have a grandchild who would have known to call me. Instead, I fell for a close variation on the theme and never suspected a thing.

He goes on. "She is accused of defrauding at least fourteen people and absconding with over a half million dollars. At this point, authorities have only found a tiny fraction of those funds." He sighs. "I'm sorry. It sounds like you may never get your $8,000 back."

"That's all right, Ethan. It would have been much worse if you hadn't raised the alarm. I'm eternally grateful to you for being my tech wizard. What I'm focused on now, instead of the money I lost, is the family I've gained. And I don't just mean my biological family – I include you and Gabe in that. You guys are my family, too."

"We feel the same toward you, *Gramasoda*," he says, his voice cracking. I hear Gabe in the background. "Let me talk to her." Then, "Grandma Sorta? We love you! We can't wait to come see you and Grams again."

"I love you guys, too," I choke out. "Let's get together again soon."

We manage to sign off without all bursting into tears and I gather myself together so I can fill Ruth in on all the details while we eat dinner.

Chapter 34

"Dana!" We hurry toward each other, arms open to experience our first physical contact since the day she was born. As we hug and rock each other, I do what I promised myself not to do – cry.

But I forgive myself, because I can feel her tears on my cheek.

"I've been dreaming of this moment for most of my life," she says as we loosen our grasps and look into each other's face.

I'd be lying if I said I've done the same, but during the past five months since fake Lisa first jolted me out of my denial mentality, my yearning to connect with my child has grown and blossomed. And here we are, mere days away from the start of a new year, finally face to face. The $8,000 mistake with Lisa seemed like an utter disaster, but look where it led me. Six months ago, I would never have dreamed of searching for my daughter. Now look at us!

Dana, Adam, and Mia spent a week around Christmas with each set of grandparents; now we've met up in Santa Fe, New Mexico for five days before both Dana and Adam have to return to work. Mia plans to meet up with some of her college friends back in Colorado to get in some skiing before classes resume a week later.

I turn to greet Adam and he embraces me in a warm hug. "This is great, Ellie. Thank you for traveling all this way to join us."

"All this way?" I say, grinning. "It was just a day's drive. I'd have traveled *anywhere* to have this opportunity to meet all of you in person!"

He steps aside and Mia steps closer, a tentative smile on her face, but her arms open for a hug. She's definitely warmed toward me since our first video call. With my acceptance that she will likely never think of me as another grandmother, I must be giving off better "vibes," as we used to say. Without that underlying pressure, she seems comfortable with approaching me as simply a friend of her parents.

Once I'm settled in my hotel room, we meet to go to dinner at one of the marvelous Mexican restaurants that Santa Fe is famous for. Tomorrow we plan to explore the Plaza, which is still decorated beautifully for the Christmas season.

"I'm hoping to find some turquoise jewelry on sale," Dana says, and I see Mia's eyes light up. Maybe I'll watch for clues on what she likes and get her something as a gift. Just because she'll probably never call me Grandma doesn't mean I don't consider her to be my one and only grandchild!

But maybe I should consult with my daughter first to make sure I'm not overstepping my role.

When our waiter brings the tab, I reach for it but Adam grabs it first. "Please," I say, "I'd like tonight's dinner to be my treat."

He shakes his head as he pulls out his wallet. "That's very kind of you, Ellie, but you are *our* guest and we're very glad you were willing to join us here."

When we reach our hotel lobby, Dana clears her throat

and nods at her daughter who nods back, then turns toward me. "Ellie," she says, pulling something from her coat pocket, "we have something we'd like to give you."

Mia holds out a small box and I take it from her. "Open it," Dana prompts.

Inside is a corded bracelet with a silver charm depicting a tree. Unlike the "tree of life" symbols I've seen, this one has no obvious trunk. It seems to grow in all directions.

"I think it looks like the tree has numerous roots as well as numerous branches," Mia explains. "It makes me think of what Mom's family tree is like – well, mine too, I guess. She has more than one root, and that makes her tree even stronger and more beautiful."

Dana leans close and speaks softly in my ear. "It's from all of us, but Mia picked it out. I think it's perfect."

"I think it's perfect, too," I say, choking up. "Thank you. Thank you so much for everything." I fasten the bracelet around my wrist and hold it up for everyone to admire.

I don't say the words out loud, but I'm thankful for their forgiveness and understanding. Dana could have resented my decision to have strangers raise her, but she doesn't. They could have rejected me as an interloper in their family, but they are accepting my friendship and love instead.

I'm one very lucky woman.

ABOUT THE AUTHOR

Diane Winger is a retired software developer who loves to seek outdoor adventures, either close by her western Colorado home or farther afield, using her Aliner camper-trailer as home base. She and her husband, Charlie, enjoy hiking, rock climbing, cross-country skiing, and kayaking, and fill their evenings with reading, writing, playing Scrabble, or planning their next trip.

She is an enthusiastic volunteer with the service organization, Altrusa International, with a particular fondness for their many literacy-enhancing projects.

Diane and Charlie are co-authors of several guidebooks on outdoor recreation. *Ellie Dwyer's Big Mistake* is Diane's 9th novel.

http://WingerBooks.com

Dear Reader,

I hope you enjoyed *Ellie Dwyer's Big Mistake*.

As an author, I thrive on feedback. You, the reader, are a major part of my inspiration to write, to explore my characters, and to try to bring them to life. So, please let me know what you liked or disliked. I'd love to hear from you. You can email me at author@WingerBooks.com, or visit me on the web at WingerBooks.com.

Just one more thing. I would consider it a great favor if you would post a review of *Ellie Dwyer's Big Mistake*. Whether you loved it or hated it, or anything in between, I appreciate your feedback. Reviews can be difficult to come by. Every review can have an enormous impact on the success or failure of a book.

You can find all of my titles on my Author Page on Amazon – the link to it is amazon.com/author/winger. Please visit my page and, if you have time, leave a review. You can also "follow" me on Amazon or on BookBub to receive news when a new title is available.

Thank you so much for reading this book and for spending time with me.

Sincerely,
Diane Winger

Also by Diane Winger

Faces
Duplicity
Rockfall
Memories & Secrets
The Daughters' Baggage
The Abandoned Girl
No Direction Home
Ellie Dwyer's Great Escape

With Charlie Winger

Highpoint Adventures
The Essential Guide to Great Sand Dunes
    National Park & Preserve
The Trad Guide to Joshua Tree

Made in the USA
San Bernardino, CA
20 April 2020